ON A TRAIN BOUND FOR NOWHERE

Susan Leigh Carlton

Susan Leigh Carlton

Tomball, TX

Susan Leigh Carlton
Tomball, TX 77377
www.susanleighcarlton.com

Publisher's Note: This is a work of fiction. Names, characters, places, and incidents are a product of the author's imagination. Locales and public names are sometimes used for atmospheric purposes. Any resemblance to actual people, living or dead, or to businesses, companies, events, institutions, or locales is completely coincidental.

On a Train Bound For Nowhere/ Susan Leigh Carlton. -- 1st ed.

Dedicated to the unfortunate children of then or now, who through no fault of their own are orphaned. Life is difficult enough with parents, let alone without them.

Orphans

*Children without families are the most vulnerable
people in the world.*

—Brooke Randolph

Description

Abandoned on the steps of a New York City Convent, when she was two months old, she was raised in the orphanage. Unadopted and nearing the maximum age for the Foundling Home, Mary Catherine is given a choice by the mother superior, and decides to take the orphan train looking for a future.

Trace Jennings is a shy young man who lost his father in the Civil War. Raised by his mother, he lives on a ranch in Helena, Montana. Raw from a disastrous mail order marriage, romance is not on his agenda.

Faced with the obstacles life has dealt them, can Mary Catherine and Trace find romance and have a life together?

Contents

Main Characters

Mary Catherine Esposito... Abandoned at two months and raised in the New York City Foundling Home.

Jonas Parsons... Owner of Thunder Canyon Ranch.

Emma Parsons... Wife of Jonas.

    Jonas... Oldest of four children.

    Martha... Mattie, oldest of the two Parsons girls

    Lettie... Youngest of the two Parsons girls

    Joshua... Youngest of the four children

Lettie Owens... Wife of the pastor of the Christian Church in Helena.

Jack Owens... Pastor and Lettie's husband.

Pearlie May... Housekeeper at Thunder Canyon Ranch.

Trace Jennings... Lives on The Lazy J Ranch. Same age as Mary Catherine. Not socially aware.

Sadie Jennings... Widow and Trace's mother.

Christine Pogue... The woman Trace met through the mail order bride newspaper.

Caleb Pogue... Christina's brother

Julia Bedford... Mary Catherine's friend at college.

Sister Louisa A kind nun at the Foundling Home.

Sister Anne A kind nun and mentor at Saint John's Hospital.

Prologue

It has been estimated there were around 30,000 orphans in New York City in 1850. This is the story of a young girl left on the steps of a convent in 1852.

The worst of the orphan situation occurred after the Civil War. One of the most gripping of New York's social problems was the abandonment of infants in the streets of the City. Poverty, immigration, inadequate housing, and a financial depression were the factors which made abandonment an ever present evil.

In 1869, it was no longer an item of news, or even of interest, to find an abandoned infant on the doorsteps of a rich family, in the hallway of a tenement, or at the entrance to a convent. St. Peter's Convent on Barclay Street was a favorite refuge of distraught mothers and very often the sisters on opening their door in the morning, would find a tiny waif deposited on the doorstep.

On October 8, 1869, the *New York Foundling Asylum of the Sisters of Charity*, in the City of New York was incorporated. Three days later, on October 11th, the Feast of the Maternity of Our Lady, Sister

Irene and her two companions, Sister Teresa Vincent and Sister Ann Aloysia, moved into a small house at 17 East 12th Street. Although they expected to spend three months in preparing for the opening of the institutions, an infant was laid at the door -step that very first night. Before January 1, 1870, the proposed opening date, they had already received 123 babies.

May 10, 1852...
No one saw her come.
No one saw her go.
No one saw anything, until the next morning when one of the sisters opened the door to Saint Peter's Convent and found the infant wrapped in a blanket made from a flower sack.

The scribbled note said, *"Il suo nome è Maria. Lei è nato il 19 Marzo. Non ho i soldi e non alimentare. Si prega di prendere cura della mia bambina."* She recognized the language as Italian but did not understand it. The mother superior read it for her.

"It says 'Her name is Maria. She was born on March 19. I have no money and no food. Please take care of my little girl.'" She made the sign of the cross. "Poor child. She must have been desperate to have to leave her baby like this. Take her to Sister Louisa in the nursery."

"What a lovely child," Sister Louisa said when she was handed the foundling, along with the note. "I will record her name as Mary Catherine Esposito. It is the Italian word for exposed."

Baby Mary Catherine was given to a small Catholic orphanage to be cared for.

CHAPTER ONE

Mary Catherine Esposito

The Mother Superior's office was void of decorations except for a small cross. Lit by a single oil lamp, the setting fit the conversation taking place.

"Is it possible for me to remain here after my birthday and work in the kitchen or help with younger children?" Mary Catherine asked.

"It is against the rules to stay beyond the eighteenth birthday, and the rules must be obeyed," the Mother said.

"What am I to do?" Mary Catherine asked. "This is the only life I've ever known. I may have a family, but I don't know who or where they are. They've certainly never come looking for me."

"You might consider entering our order," Mother Louisa suggested.

"It is not something I think I could do," Mary Catherine said.

"One does have to be called," Mother Louisa admitted.

"I don't feel I have such a calling," Mary Catherine said. "What became of the others that have left?"

"Sadly, we don't know. I pray the Heavenly Father watches over them and keeps them safe, but we must also realize that His will must be done."

"It doesn't seem right to bring us in off the streets only to throw us back when we are eighteen."

"It is not as callous as that," she said. "We try to help them find work, and some of them marry. You will have the advantages of a good education when you leave. Think of the many who can neither read or write. You've worked hard and been a good student. You will be fine."

Two days later...

"I have something that may help you. There is a mercy train leaving tomorrow," Mother Louisa told Mary Catherine. "It is sponsored by the Church's Orphan Society. Would you like to be on it?"

"How does it work, and where is it going?" she asked

"It is going to Montana, but will stop at several places along the way. Those places will be notified and families wishing to adopt a child can apply to do so from the children on the train."

"Do all of the children get adopted?" Mary Catherine asked.

"I don't have any information on that, but I would assume they would remain under the care of the Church if they aren't."

"I will go. There's no hope for me here. I might as well be hopeless someplace else as on the streets of New York.."

"My child, you must always remember, what happens is God's plan."

"I have trouble understanding any plan that would have my mother leaving me on the doorsteps of the convent."

"It was part of His plan to have you cared for," Mother Louisa said.

"Then why did He allow me to be born to a mother who couldn't or wouldn't care for me?"

"We don't always understand the ways of the Heavenly Father."

"I surely don't," Mary Catherine said.

* * *

The train station was darker than the orphanage. The smoke from the trains hung in the air like a fog rolling in from the ocean. Soot clung to everything.

The nuns herded the children together to board the train. The oldest of the children were in a wooden car with seats. The infants were in a car with the nuns.

Mary Catherine was the oldest of forty-five orphans on the Mercy Train when it left New York City. Three nuns were also on the train to care for the infant children. As the oldest, Mary Catherine had the responsibility to help in the care of the other children.

The trip was a new adventure for the older children, including Mary Catherine, who had never been out of Manhattan. When her responsibilities permitted she stared at the passing countryside, as they traveled through the mountains of Pennsylvania, through Ohio and into Indiana. She saw the farmers in their fields and the small clapboard houses they lived in. The streets of the cities were clogged with horses and wagons.

The plains of Kansas and Nebraska were boring, except for the occasions when the tracks ran alongside the wagon paths taken by the wagon trains.

"I wonder how far those people have walked," Mary Catherine asked one of the nuns.

"We travel further in one hour than they travel in a day," the nun replied. "I have read where their journey lasts for six months or more."

"They look tired, but at least they have something at the end of their trip, where I have nothing."

"They are going into an unknown, just as you are. They do not know any more about what awaits them than you know what awaits you. It is hope, and faith that keeps them going."

"Faith and hope," Mary Catherine said. "Two things I have very little of to carry me."

"God will provide," the nun said, with a benign smile. "You must have faith."

"It is hard, Sister. It seems as if I'm on a train to nowhere."

Cheyenne, Wyoming...

The train neared the small frontier town in Wyoming.

The newly scrubbed orphans had been checked to make sure they were wearing clean clothes before the train reached Cheyenne. Mary Catherine attended to the others before changing to her other dress, and scrubbing her own face.

The train shuddered to a stop. It was a cloudless day with no wind. The cinders and smoke spewed from the stack like a dark cloud over the depot. The children walked to the wooden platform and lined up to face the farmers and ranchers who had submitted applications for adoption.

The prospective parents poked and prodded the children, checking their teeth, arms, and legs, in much the same manner they would had they been selecting cattle.

After an hour, fifteen of the children had been chosen for adoption. Most of them were the older boys, since they could immediately provide much needed help on the ranches and farms. Three infants were also chosen, and were clutched tightly in the arms of their new mothers. Those not selected, including Mary Catherine, were herded back to the train and taken to the next stop, which was Laramie. She changed back to her other dress.

I'm glad for those who were picked, but I got what I expected... nothing.

The sisters were pleased with the outcome of the stop. It had been successful in their eyes with fifteen of their charges having been placed.

The process was repeated at the next two stops. After stopping in Billings, the train arrived in Helena with only three orphans remaining, all of them girls. One of them was Mary Catherine.

CHAPTER TWO

Trace Jennings

Cort Jennings entered the war late. He volunteered and was assigned to the 34th Indiana Veteran Volunteer Infantry Regiment in their southwest campaign. He was killed in action on May 12, 1865, five weeks after the war ended when General Robert E. Lee surrendered to General Grant of the Union Army at Appomattox Courthouse on April 9th, 1865.

News of the end of hostilities reached Helena by telegraph late in the morning the next day.

Trace had been fourteen years old when his father told his mother, Sadie about his belated decision to fight for the Union.

"Why?" she had asked. "We're not even part of the Union."

"We were part of it when we were in Indiana. The time will come when Dakota Territory will become a state. It's my beholden duty to go, and it's something I should have done back when it started."

"What about us," she asked. "What about what we have here? Aren't we worth fighting for?"

"I feel that is what I'll be doing. I'm sorry, Sadie, but sometimes a man's got to do what he's got to do. I've spoken to our neighbors and they've promised to look out for you and Trace until I get back."

"And what if you don't come back?" she asked.

"Trace is a man now. He'll see to you."

"I want to go with you, Pa," Trace said. "I can shoot as good as you can."

"You can," and that's why I need for you to stay here and take care of your Ma. The Lakota's are quiet, but she still needs a man around. Now I don't want any more arguing about this. It's settled, and I'll be leaving the day after tomorrow."

Two days later, just after sunup, he set out on his way to war. It was the last time they would see him.

* * *

Saturday, April 14, 1865...

Silas Farmer, owner of the general store greeted them when they came in. "Morning Miz Jennings. I haven't seen you two in here in a long time."

"It has been a long time, almost two months," she said. "We've run out of just about everything, so I have a long list."

"I'll bet you were excited by the news weren't you?"

"What news?"

"The war is over. You mean you didn't hear about it?"

"No, we don't get many visitors to the ranch, so we haven't heard. When did it happen?"

"Last Sunday. General Lee surrendered to General Grant. I guess Cort will be coming home any day now."

"Oh Lordy, I never thought I would live to see the day," she said, fanning herself with the back of her hand. "He's coming back."

"Howdy, Mr. Farmer," Trace said. "How have you been?"

"The war's over, your papa is coming home," his mother interrupted.

His face lit up. "When?"

"Well, I don't rightly know. Silas said it ended last Sunday, so however long it takes him to get back from wherever he is."

A month later…

Trace looked down the trail his father would be taking home. There had been no word from him. On a Wednesday, just before lunch, a carriage stopped in front of the main house.

"Hello the house," the driver called out.

"Preacher! What brings you and Miss Lettie so far out of town," Trace asked as he came around the corner of the house.

"We need to talk to your mother," Lettie Owens said in a voice Trace had long decided must be the way an angel sounded.

"Come on in, I'll tell her you're here."

He stamped his boots on the porch, opened the door, and stepped aside to let them enter. He climbed the stairs and went to the sewing room. "Ma, Miss Lettie and the preacher are here and want to see you."

"Well land sakes, you didn't leave them standing outside did you?"

"No ma'am," he said. "They're in the parlor."

She glanced in the mirror and ran her fingers through her hair to smooth out the strays that had escaped her bun.

"It's so good to see you," she exclaimed, wiping her hand on her faded apron. "I look a fright, but I've been mending all day. Trace goes through the knees of his pants like they were paper. What brings you so far out of town?"

"I'll go on back to the corral," Trace said. It's good to see you."

"You need to stay," Jack said. "This concerns you too."

"It sounds serious," Sadie said frowning.

"Sadie, you had better sit down," Lettie said, moving to make room beside her on the sofa. "The news just came in last night. Cort was killed May 12, in Texas near the Mexican border."

"It can't be. The war ended over a month ago. We have been looking for him to show up."

"It's true," Jack said. "It was at a place called Palmita Ranch near Brownsville."

"I'm very sorry for your loss," Lettie said, her eyes moist with the sadness she felt. "It came in by telegraph last night, too late to bring out, so we told them we would come tell you this morning. I have the printed copy here." She handed Sadie a piece of paper containing the scribblings of the telegrapher.

"It was a total waste of his life," Sadie said. "I tried to convince him not to go, but he wouldn't listen. Said it was his duty. Now he's dead."

"If there is anything we can do, or anything you need, please let us know."

"Will they be bringing him here to be buried?" Sadie asked.

"There was nothing in the wire about the disposition of those killed in action," Jack said. "There were thirty names on the list. It would be my guess they were buried where they fell."

"So all we will have is his memory," Sadie said.

"His soul left the body and ascended into heaven when he died, he is waiting for you there," Lettie told her.

"He should have let me go with him," Trace said. "It might have made a difference."

"And then I might have lost both of you. I would be alone now. He knew what he was doing when he made you stay.

"You are the man of the house," Sadie said to her son. He had just turned eighteen.

CHAPTER THREE

Helena

Mary Catherine was given space in Saint John's nunnery since she was the only unadopted orphan on the train.

"You have several options while you are here," the mother superior told her. "I would expect you to help in the hospital as a nurse's aide. There is no pay for this, but you will have a place to sleep and food.

"You can try to find work in one of the local businesses or one of the local families. You will not be forced onto the street. Have you given any thought to the future?"

"I guess I haven't," Mary Catherine said. "I've been so discouraged by not being wanted, I can hardly think of anything else.

"I'm good with children, and I have a good education, but I don't know how to put it to use. I've had no contact with anyone outside the orphanage in New York City."

"I think it would be wise for you to work in the hospital. This will put you in contact with some of the local citizens and give you some experience in the social aspect of life."

"At least I will be doing something. When do I start?"

"I will have someone get suitable clothes for you and you can start tomorrow, by accompanying one of the sisters in the hospital to see what is needed."

The next morning...

Mary Catherine began her day by attending mass. The mother superior introduced her to Sister Anne. "Mary Catherine is going to be helping us in the hospital until she decides what she is going to do. I would like for you to help her get started."

"Mary Catherine is a beautiful name," Sister Anne said. "I am blessed to meet you."

"Thank you," Mary Catherine said. "It was given to me at the New York Foundling Home."

"You were on the train?"

"Yes, but no one wanted me, so Mother Superior was kind enough to take me in. I should tell you, I have no experience with anything except children. I seem to have a way with them."

"We occasionally have child patients. It is always difficult to see one of them in pain." She quickly crossed herself. "Are you thinking about joining the order?"

"I don't have the kind of faith and dedication I would need to join," Mary Catherine said.

"The doctor will be here around eight o'clock to check on his patients. We'll go with him while he does his rounds. Before then, we will take their meals to them, and at the same time, see to their personal needs."

"How many patients are there?"

"We have forty beds. Most of them are in wards, and usually not all of them are occupied. Let's begin, shall we?"

"Are there any children in the hospital?"

"Not at this time. We don't get many, and there is not much we can do for them when they are here. Most of our patients are here because of accidents on the ranches, and involve broken arms and legs. An occasional shooting but that is all. Most babies are delivered at home by midwives. A doctor is usually not involved unless there are complications. If surgery is required, he has them brought here.

"We have to remember our patients do not usually want to be here. They are often in pain and are not at their best, so we must try to make their stay as pleasant as possible. Put yourself in their place, and remember the golden rule. Treat them as you would want to be treated if you were in their position."

Living in the nunnery was bleak. Conversation was limited and it was quiet as a tomb. Mary Catherine was determined to find something else as soon as possible. What she didn't know was how to go about it. She was reluctant to speak to anyone she didn't know, and even when speaking to patients, she was at a loss what to say.

"Are you troubled?" Sister Anne asked.

Mary Catherine shook her head. "I don't know what's wrong. I don't know what I expected, but this isn't it. I can't seem to get interested in anything. I don't see any point to what I'm doing."

"How old are you?"

"I'll be eighteen in two months."

"Why you're still a child. You have a lot to look forward to in life."

"Sister Anne, I have nothing. I have no clothes, no friends... nothing."

"I consider you to be my friend," Sister Anne said.

"You are, but you know what I mean. I see the people that come in here, talking about what they have been doing, or planning to do. Do you know I have never talked to anyone outside of the orphanage, or the hospital?"

"I don't mean to be critical, but have you ever tried to start a conversation with anyone here?"

"No ma'am, I guess I haven't," Mary Catherine replied.

"Let's go check on Mr. Chandler," Sister Anne said.

She stopped outside the room. "Mr. Chandler has a cattle ranch outside of town. He likes to talk, and he's a funny man. If he asks you anything, and he will, answer him. It will get him started. I'll introduce you. "

"Mr. Chandler, what have you been up to today?" she asked.

"Just chasing the nurses," he said. "Haven't caught one yet though. Can't run much with this cast on my leg."

"Has the doctor been in yet?" she asked.

"I think he's dodging me. He thinks I've lost my senses."

"Mr. Chandler, this is Mary Catherine Esposito. The Heavenly Father sent her to help us take care of you."

"It's about time he sent someone not wearing a habit. You're too pretty to be in an ugly place like Saint John's. Where are you from?"

"New York City," Mary Catherine said, her voice barely a whisper.

"You are going to have to speak up, I'm an old codger and my hearing ain't what it used to be."

"Tell Mary Catherine how you broke your leg," Sister Anne said.

"There you go again, Sister Anne, I didn't break my leg. That danged horse did. I'm going to have to set you straight again."

He looked at Mary Catherine. "Drag a chair over and I'll tell you true."

She looked at Sister Anne, who nodded and smiled. She pulled the chair over, and sat by the bed.

You ever heard tell there ain't a horse that can't be rode, and there ain't a man that can't be throwed?"

"No sir."

"I proved part of it true myself. That danged horse throwed me against the corral fence."

"Is that how you broke your leg?"

"Girl, you got to pay more attention. I didn't break my leg. The danged horse did."

"When you hit the fence?"

"No, I been throwed a lot, and I know how to fall. I figgered I'd show him who was boss, so I had two of the hands hold him while I got back in the saddle.

"I thought I'd convinced him because he just stood there. I raked him with my spurs, and he commenced to jumping like nothing you ever seen. The cowboys was all a yelling and a whistling whilst I was holding on, and I was doing pretty good at it too. He reared up and pawed his front legs like he was trying to rake the clouds down on me. He stood so tall, he fell over backwards, throwing me again, and then he fell on top of me. That's how that danged horse come to break my leg. In two places too. It hurt me some, so I decided to take a little nap whilst the boys brought me here."

Mary Catherine had been enthralled by the story. "It must have been terrible for you," she said.

"Darlin, it warn't near as bad as it's going to be for that danged horse when I get out of here."

"Are you going to shoot him?" she asked, a look of horror on her face.

"Shoot him? 'Course not. I'm going to ride him to a standstill and then laugh in his face. And that's the truth of the matter."

The most beautiful woman Mary Catherine had ever seen walked into the room. "Sam, are you still telling those tall tales of yours?" She bent and kissed him on the cheek.

"I'm Lettie Owens," she said. "My husband is pastor of the Christian Church here. "Sam is one of our most incorrigible members. He's an old reprobate, but we love him."

"Glory be," Sam said. "That danged horse needs to break my leg more often. Here I am, all stove up in unbearable pain and I got two of the prettiest of all of God's women here to watch over me.

"This here's Mary Catherine, and she came all the way from New York City to see me."

"I'm pleased to meet you, Mary Catherine," Lettie said.

"Thank you," Mary Catherine said. "It's my pleasure."

"I been trying for two or three years to get Lettie to leave Jack and marry up with me," Sam said. "I figgered I was making progress until that danged horse broke my leg."

"Sam, you're incorrigible," Lettie said. "I have others more deserving than you to visit. Mary Catherine, we'll talk again and be sure to stay out of his reach." She kissed Sam on the cheek, touched Mary Catherine on the shoulder and walked from the room.

"There goes one of the best people you will ever meet," Sam said soberly. "We all feel she has a straight line to Heaven and is one of God's angels sent to watch over us. With Lettie praying for you, you can feel sure of a good outcome."

"That was beautiful, Mr. Sam. Thank you. Now I had better get back to work."

CHAPTER FOUR

The Last Battle

"We had some bad news this morning," Sadie said, to the ranch hands gathered in front of the barn. "The preacher and his wife told us a wire came in yesterday with casualties. Cort's name was listed among the dead. He was killed in Texas on May 12th. Since the war had ended over a month ago, we were expecting him home any day. They said it was the last battle of the war.

"We will continue to operate the ranch as usual. I want you to know we are in good condition and we will continue to fill our contracts with your help. Newt will continue as foreman, and Trace will assume the role his father played. Newt has full hiring and firing authority the same as he has since Cort left." She choked on the words and regained her composure. "If any of you are concerned about the future and want to leave, let Newt know and he will see that you get what you have coming to you. Does anyone have any questions?"

"Miss Sadie," Newt asked, "Will they be bringing him home?"

"We don't know, but I don't think so. I'm going to write the War Department and ask about it. Texas is a long way off though."

A lanky cowboy pushed his hat back, revealing his dark curly hair. "Miss Sadie, We're all sorry for you and Trace. Don't you worry about things. We won't let you down."

"Thank you Curly, I appreciate it. That was all I had to say. We are planning a memorial service in the church, and you're all welcome to be there. It will be a week from Sunday."

* * *

Sam's Room...

"Howdy Jack," Sam greeted him. "Doc just told me he is finally going to let me out of here."

"I'm sure the nurses will be relieved to hear that," Jack said.

"You must be Mary Catherine," Jack said to the girl standing by the bedside. "You're the one from New York, aren't you? Lettie told me about you. Welcome to Helena."

"Thank you. She's been very nice to me." *That sounded dumb, but at least I said something.*

"I'm letting you out only if you promise to stop the bronc busting," Doctor Palmer said. "I don't want you breaking another leg and messing up my work. We might not be able to save it next time."

"I told you I didn't do it, the danged clumsy horse did it when he fell on me."

The doctor laughed. "Sam regardless of what you think, a sixty year old man has no business trying to break a horse. Your bones are brittle and break easier than they did forty years ago."

"Doc, you didn't have to say how old I was in front of my new girl here."

"Sam, did you hear about Cort Jennings?" Jack asked.

"What about Cort? Is he home?" Sam asked.

"No," Jack said. "He won't be coming home. He was killed down in Texas. It was the last battle of the war, over a month after it was supposed to end. The list with his name came in a few days ago. Lettie and I went to tell Sadie and Trace about it."

"Dang it all," Sam said. "Cort was a good man, and a good neighbor."

"How did Sadie take it?" Doc asked.

"They both took it hard, I think it hit Trace harder than it did his mother," Jack said. "She's a strong woman.

"We're going to have a memorial service for him Sunday afternoon."

"I'll be there," Sam said.

"I'm not sure it's a good idea for you to move around much until you've had more time to heal."

"Cort was my friend, and so is Sadie. I will be there," Sam said adamantly.

"Just be careful and don't overdo it."

* * *

"Would it be appropriate for me to go to the memorial service?" Mary Catherine asked Sister Anne. "Mr. Sam thinks a lot of him. I met Miss Lettie and I'd like to see her again too."

"Lettie Owens is a kind and generous person with a very strong faith. We are blessed to have her in our town."

"Would you like to go with me?" Mary Catherine asked. "Are you allowed to go to a Christian church?"

"We all love and worship the same God, so it is permitted, and I would like to go."

The church was nearly half full when they arrived. Lettie excused herself from the group she was with and approached them. "I'm so glad you came," she said, taking one of each of their hands. "His wife and son are in the front pew. I'll introduce you, if you like."

"Sadie, I would like for you to meet Sister Anne and Mary Catherine from the hospital. This is Sadie Jennings."

"Thank you for coming," Sadie said. "This is our... my son Trace." Trace looked to be about Mary Catherine's age.. Wearing a distressed look, he stared at the floor, and mumbled something.

Shocking herself, Mary Catherine reached out and touched his arm. "I'm so sorry," she said. "I can't pretend to know how you feel, because I never knew my father or mother."

"Mr. Sam told us about your husband," Sister Anne said, crossing herself. "It must have come as a shock to lose your him so long after the war ended."

"It was," Sadie said. "We had been looking for him to come down the road when Jack and Lettie brought us the news.

"Are you new to Helena?" she asked Mary Catherine?"

"Yes ma'am. I came on the mercy train from New York City."

"Are you going to be a nun?" Sadie asked, before she realized the personal nature of her question. "I am sorry," she said. "I shouldn't have asked such a personal question."

"It's all right," Mary Catherine said. "I don't know what I am going to do yet."

Jack Owens had taken his place at the altar. "We had better find a seat," Sister Anne said.

"Why don't you sit with us?" Sadie asked.

"Thank you," Sister Anne said. "I would like that."

After the services concluded, and they left the church, Sam Chandler hobbled up using crutches, accompanied by a tall, suntanned man wearing a white Stetson hat. He wobbled as he hugged Sadie. After shaking Trace's hand, he said, "Cort was a good man, and I'm going to miss him. You always knew where you stood with him, and I appreciated it. We're all going to miss him."

"He felt the same way about you, Sam," Sadie said.

"Sister Anne, I guess I shouldn't be surprised to see you here," Sam said. "I'm pleased you brought Mary Catherine. I miss having someone to listen to me ramble at night. It's good to see you again," he said to Mary Catherine."

"You too, Mr. Sam. Have you been taking it easy like the doctor said?"

"I ain't been near that danged horse if that's what you mean."

"Good for you," she replied.

"Don't take that to mean I ain't going to get even with him."

"Just make sure you wind up on top," she said.

The man with Sam laughed aloud. "You don't have to worry about that," Sam said. "This here's Clint Weathers, my foreman. Clint and his wife, Maude watch me like a hawk watches a rabbit."

Clint touched the brim of his hat. "Pleased to meet you, ma'am."

"I have to be getting back to the hospital," Mary Catherine said. "You take care, Mr. Sam. Mr. Weathers, Trace, Miss Sadie, it's been nice meeting you."

They walked down the board sidewalk toward the hospital. "I am really proud of you," Sister Anne said. "You did very well. It's nice to see you coming out of your shell."

"I appreciate that, Sister. I do feel better about things. Talking to Mr. Sam has helped me a lot."

CHAPTER FIVE

Lettie and Mary C

"Miss Lettie, I would like to talk to you when you have the time," Mary Catherine said. "It's something I wouldn't feel comfortable talking to the sisters about."

"Of course," Lettie said. "We can talk in the chapel here, or you are welcome to come to my house if you would be more comfortable."

"I don't want to put you to any trouble," Mary Catherine said. "I haven't done anything wrong, but the Church has done so much for me, I feel guilty for even thinking this way."

"I'm sure any guilt you feel is self-imposed. Can you get away and have lunch or dinner with me, or with us?"

"I've been helping out during the daytime because there's more to do then."

"Can you have dinner with us tonight?" Lettie asked.

"I don't want to deceive anyone," Mary Catherine said.

"This isn't deceptive. I consider you to be a friend, and as such, I've invited you to dinner."

It weighed on her conscience all afternoon. She decided not to carry the guilt any longer, and went to the Mother Superior's small office.

"Mother, may I speak to you for a minute please?"

"Yes of course, my child. Are you troubled?"

"No... yes. I asked Miss Lettie Owens if I could talk to her, and she invited me to dinner. I don't know if I did the right thing."

"Sister Anne has told me you're changing and in the way we hoped. Remember, when you first came, I told you needed to decide the direction you wished to take in life?"

"Yes, Mother. I remember, and I haven't made any progress in that direction. It's one reason I wanted to speak to Miss Lettie."

"We would like for you to dedicate yourself to the Church, but it is not something we can decide for you. It must be your choice, and if anyone has tried to push you toward that, then they are misguided."

"No one has put any pressure on me, but the Church has done so much for me, I feel it is a debt I owe, and I have nothing to pay with except myself."

"The only debt you have is to yourself. Some are chosen to take our path, but it only when it is part of God's plan. You would feel it in your heart if it were right for you. You should talk to Mrs. Owens and anyone else you want. She is a devoted child of God who serves in her own way, and so should you. There is a place for everyone.

"I am pleased you felt the need to discuss this with me, and were comfortable enough to do so. You go with our blessing.

Later...

"Come in, and welcome to our home," Lettie said. "Would you like some refreshment? I have tea and lemonade, and I could make coffee."

"I'm fine, Miss Lettie. By the way, I spoke to the Mother Superior about coming. I felt I owed them."

"Oh?"

"She encouraged it. We had a nice talk. She said almost the same thing you said.

"Why don't we go into the kitchen while I finish cooking? Jack is working on his sermon, and then we can talk after dinner."

"It smells wonderful in here! Is there anything I can do to help? I can't cook, but I did help in the orphanage."

"You can set the table if you like," Lettie said. She pointed to the cabinets where the dishes and eating utensils were kept.

Sensing Mary Catherine's lack of experience, Lettie said, "We will only need plates, spoons and forks, and table knives. Jack and I will have tea, so glasses for us, and whatever you need."

"I am a nosy person by nature, you don't need to answer if you prefer not to. How did you lose your parents?"

"I don't know. I was left on the doorstep of the convent, with a note giving my name as Mary. No one knows any more than that, at least I don't know of anyone that does."

"That is so sad," Lettie said.

"I've accepted that I was unwanted. Proof of it is that I was never adopted. I was getting close to the age limit for the Foundling Home, so I asked to be allowed to go with the mercy train. I didn't want to go out on my own in New York City."

"Have you ever thought about how hard it must have been for your mother to give you up? Maybe she knew she couldn't take care of you and was willing to make the sacrifice for you."

"Anytime I had those thoughts they were chased away by the fact she could have visited me anytime."

""That would have been doubly hard," Lettie said.

"Miss Lettie, do you always try to find some good in everything?"

"I do. I have a very strong faith, and I believe there is a plan, but I also believe we have to make choices as we live our lives. I also believe in prayer and that our prayers are answered. Maybe the answer we receive is not the one we want, but they are answered.

"If you will put the food out, I'll let Jack know it's ready," Lettie said.

Jack offered thanks for the food and asked for a blessing for their guest.

Food in the orphanage had been plain and in short supply. The food at the nunnery was more plentiful, but bland. Lettie was as good a cook as she was at everything else.

"Miss Lettie, I have never had a meal as good as this," Mary Catherine said.

"Thank you, dear. Eat hearty, we have plenty as you can see."

"You girls go ahead and have your talk, I'll take care of the kitchen," Jack said.

"You have such an interesting life," Mary Catherine said. "I envy you."

"Jack and I are well and truly blessed," Lettie said. "The Lord has provided for us. What did you want to talk about?"

"Me. I don't believe I am suited to become a nun. I respect them for their faith and what they do, but I want more for myself."

"What do you want for yourself?"

"I want to be like ordinary people. People like you. The only clothes I have are the ones I had from the orphanage, and the clothes I wear at the hospital. I have no income, so I can't buy anything. I do get a place to sleep and meals, but that is it. I'm not complaining, and I'm grateful for what I have.

"I am not afraid of work, but I have no experience at doing anything. I am good with children, and I can read and write, but that is it.

"Sister Anne has encouraged me to be more outgoing, and I'm trying to do that. I just don't know what else I should do."

"Do you want to keep working at the hospital?" Lettie asked.

"I like to think I'm helping, but I would like to do something where I get paid."

"I might be able to help with part of your problem now," Lettie said, "but I'll have to think about the rest.

"We have a very generous congregation and many of them have donated various things to help others. Let's go see what I have."

She led the way to a room used for storage. "There are a few dresses here that were donated. You might be able to find something among them that will fit."

She found two that fit well.

"Miss Lettie, I can't tell you how much I appreciate this."

"Don't give it another thought," Lettie said. "I'm glad you found something."

CHAPTER SIX

The Passing of Time

Sadie Jennings wrote to the War Department asking for information on the disposition of Cort's remains. Two months later, she received a letter from the office of Edwin Stanton, Secretary of War.

Our records indicate Courtland Robert Jennings was killed in action on May 12, 1865 during. He was interred with the other casualties on Palmita Ranch near Brownsville, Texas.

The Secretary extends his condolences for your loss.

"This is probably all we will ever get," Sadie told Trace. It's senseless. He died for a lost cause that had been over for a month. I don't know where I will put this, but I'm going to get a frame for it."

"I still can't believe he's not coming home," Trace said. "When we heard the war was over, I quit using his stall, and cleaned it all out so it would be ready for him. I think I'm going to put Blue in there."

"He would want you to use it. He worked hard to make this place what it is. When we first came to Montana, we lived in a soddy. It was not much more than a lean-to. Now we have one of the finest ranches in the area. He was very proud of what he had done.

"We used to get in that old buckboard and just ride the line. He would talk about what he wanted to do, and then he did it. Now it's yours to take it on from here."

"I can never fill his shoes, Ma."

"You don't have to. He was as proud of you as he was the ranch. Many's the time we'd be sitting on the porch or lying in bed and he would say, 'Sade, we have a mighty fine boy. I wish Pap could have seen him.' He always called me Sade. He was a fine figger of a man and was the catch of the county back in Ohio. Lord, I loved that man." She wiped her eyes on her apron. "You don't want to hear an old woman's rumbling on about the past."

"I do," Trace said. "We'd be in the barn milking, and you'd come out on the porch. He would just stop and watch until you moved out of sight. He'd say 'I hope you do as good as I did, when it comes time for you to find a wife.'

"I best get on with my chores. I don't want Newt to think I'm slacking off."

"When are you going to find yourself a girl? A boy your age should have one."

"I'm only nineteen. I got plenty of time," he said.

"Your pa thought he had plenty of time too. Don't put it off. You never know when you're going to be struck down."

"How many girls have you seen around here?"

"Not many, I admit, but there was that girl at the service."

"I don't even know her name," he said.

"Mary Catherine. Her name was Mary Catherine."

"Did you see who she was with? A nun. She's Catholic."

"So? She's a girl. A right pretty girl too."

* * *

Saturday, the parsonage...

"Emma, did you ever hire anyone to help with the kids?" Lettie asked.

Emma Parsons was married to the owner of the Thunder Canyon Ranch. With four young children, she had her hands full. "We haven't found anyone I thought could handle it. I'm probably being a little too particular, but I don't want to settle for someone who won't be good for the children. Why do you ask?"

"I know someone who might interest you."

"Do you have another widow lady?" Emma asked. Lettie was well known for helping widows in dire straits.

Lettie's smile lit the room. "She's not a widow, she is new in town, but I've been very impressed with her. It's a sad story. She is from New York City and was abandoned shortly after she was born. She has never known her mother or father. Right now, she is living in the nunnery and helps in the hospital in exchange for her room and board."

"From New York? How did she land in Helena?" Emma asked.

"She came in on an orphan train and was the only one not adopted. She literally had nothing but the clothes on her back and was wearing what the sisters had given her. I had some donations and was able to give her two dresses. She asked to be on the train because she was approaching the maximum age for the Foundling Home, and didn't want to be on the streets of New York City."

"Couldn't she have joined the sisters?"

"She could have, but doesn't think it would be right for her. She came to me last week for advice."

"Can she read and write?" Emma asked.

"Yes, both. She's been helping with the hospital patients and wherever she can. She's had a hard life, and I would like to help her if possible."

"Can you arrange for us to meet her? We're going back home tomorrow after the service."

Lettie found Mary Catherine in the large ward at the hospital. When she was finished, she saw Lettie and joined her.

"Hi," she said. "I haven't seen you here on a Saturday before."

"I came to see you," Lettie said. "There's a couple I would like for you to meet. Can you come to dinner tonight?"

"I think so," she said. "I'm nearly finished here and it's been pretty quiet."

"You'll like them. Their names are Jonas and Emma Parsons. Jonas has a large ranch between here and Spring Hill, and Emma is a school teacher. Why don't you come over after you're finished here and we'll make an evening of it?"

"I would like that. Will six o'clock be all right?"

"Come earlier if you like."

"I'll get cleaned up and should be there between five and six. Thank you Miss Lettie. I'm looking forward to it."

CHAPTER SEVEN

Would You Consider

"Good to see you again, Mary Catherine," Jack said, answering the door. "Come in, they're in the parlor."

"Thank you, Mr. Jack." She followed him into the parlor.

Jack did the introductions. "Emma, Jonas, this is Mary Catherine Esposito. They have a ranch between here and Spring Hill."

She was embarrassed by being the center of attention. "I'm glad to meet you," she said softly.

"Emma is one of our mail order brides," Lettie said.

"I don't know what that is," Mary Catherine said.

"I advertised for a wife in a newspaper," Jonas said, "and Emma answered the ad. We exchanged several letters and she agreed to come meet me."

Lettie and Jack knew the story, and smiled at the memory. "Tell her what happened," Lettie urged.

"It was a long train ride, an eighteen day trip by riverboat, and a very rough ride in a stagecoach. When I got to Spring Hill, there was no one to meet me, so I stayed in the hotel that night. The next morning, there was no sign of anyone looking for me so I ventured out and met the storekeeper who knew I was coming. He sent me to see Mattie and Will Tucker at the church. They were surprised I hadn't been met, and took me to the ranch to find him. When we got there, we found he had been badly hurt in a stampede and was here in Saint John's Hospital, so we came here. This is where I met Lettie and Jack. Jonas's first words to me ordered me from his rooms."

"Be fair," Jonas said. "I thought Carter was going to amputate my leg and I didn't want to saddle you with a cripple. Besides, I didn't even know you were coming."

"Anyway to end a long and almost pointless story, here we are, happily married, with four children."

"That is an interesting story," Mary Catherine said.

"It is beyond the normal, I have to admit," Emma said. "I guess you're wondering why Lettie dragged you over here to meet two strangers."

"No ma'am. She didn't drag me over here. She asked me to come, and I don't see how anyone could ever turn Miss Lettie down for anything."

"How well I know that," Emma said. "For some months now, Jonas and I have been looking for someone to help me with the children, but so far, we have been unable to find someone satisfactory. This would be a paid position and include room and board. We have a housekeeper, but with her other responsibilities, she doesn't have enough time to do much with them. The oldest and youngest are boys with the two girls in between.

"Lettie told me about your situation. Are you interested in meeting them, and then talking about it?"

"Yes ma'am," Mary Catherine said. "I'm pretty good with children. I was the oldest girl in the orphanage and helped the sisters with the others."

"I would suggest you return to the ranch with us and meet them. If you are compatible, and want to try it, then we go from there. If it doesn't work, we'll pay you for your time and bring you back to Helena. How does that sound to you?"

"It sounds wonderful," Mary Catherine said. "I would really like to do it. It's an answer to my prayers." She turned, "Miss Lettie, I don't know how to thank you for your help."

"It's my pleasure to help," Lettie said.

"Mary Catherine, Jonas took me to Paris on our honeymoon, but we didn't spend much time in New York City. What is it like?"

"I don't know. The only time I was out of Manhattan was when I rode on the orphan train. We never went away from the orphanage."

"I'm sorry," Emma said. "It was thoughtless of me to ask such a question."

"It's all right. You didn't know."

"What was it like for you?"

"It was quiet, because the nuns were very strict, but they had to be because there were so many of us. There was not enough food sometimes. There's more at the nunnery, but it is very plain. We didn't complain because we were grateful for what we had."

"Were many children adopted from there?"

"No ma'am. They came in faster than they left. That's why they started up the mercy trains. There was a train just about every week, but I don't think most of them came this far."

"They couldn't have, because we have had train service only about four years," Jonas said.

"Do you sew?" Emma asked.

"Some. I used to mend our clothes. I've never made anything new."

You've never had anything new either, have you.

"Look at the time," Emma said. "I didn't realize it had gotten so late.

"Will you join us for church tomorrow? We plan to have lunch right after, and then leave for the ranch. It's over an hour's ride. Will that give you enough time?"

"Ma'am, I owe it to the sisters to attend early Mass since I'll be leaving right after."

"If you're ready, we'll drop you off. I don't think you should be walking alone this late in the evening," Jonas said.

"I'll be all right," Mary Catherine said. "I want to help Miss Lettie with the kitchen."

"That isn't necessary, dear. Jonas is right. You shouldn't be walking alone, especially on a Saturday night."

CHAPTER EIGHT

A New Beginning

The Lazy J...

"What does her being Catholic have to do with anything?" Sadie asked.

"Nothing, I guess," he said.

"I think you should talk to her," Sadie said.

"I've only seen her one time and now you want me to marry her. It isn't done that way, Ma."

"How do you know how it's done?"

"I just know. I'm not in any hurry to get married. I want to enjoy things."

"You don't do anything except work. What are you enjoying? Tell me that."

"I'm learning, Ma. I'm learning a lot from Newt."

"So how many wives does he have?"

"He's not interested in having a wife," Trace said.

"He spends half of his wages on the fancy girls and the rest he wastes," Sadie said. "I better not hear about you going upstairs in the saloon. In fact, I better not hear of you going in the saloon."

Aw, Ma."

Sunday...

"Lettie, the girl that was at the memorial, is she still around?" Sadie asked.

"You mean Mary Catherine?"

"Mary Catherine... that's the one. Is she still at the hospital?"

"No, she started working for Emma Parsons as a nanny."

"I don't believe I know her," Sadie said.

"They have a ranch near Spring Hill, why do you ask?"

"She's about the same age as Trace, and I thought they might make a nice couple."

"I don't know about that. She's very shy around people, but she is a sweet girl."

"It was just a thought. Do they come to church?"

"Emma and Jonas do most of their shopping in Spring Hill. They come to Helena every couple of months, and they do come to services when they're in town."

"I'm worried about Trace. Since we got the word about Cort, he's hardly left the ranch. I think he would live in the bunkhouse if I'd let him."

"I've never seen him at any of the socials we have for our young folks on Friday nights," Lettie said.

"Who comes to those?"

"Most of the high school youth," Lettie said.

"They're too young for him then. He wouldn't have anything to do with them."

"That's too bad. It's a good way to meet some of the others in town. We have ice cream, and music. Some of the kids dance." She laughed, "Most of the time, it's girls dancing with girls though."

"What did we do when we were that age?" Sadie asked.

"Went to bed early, got up early and went to church on Sunday," Lettie said. "About the same as they do now, except not enough of them come on Sunday."

"I don't know what I'm going to do."

"I wouldn't worry about it. He is still a young boy," Lettie told her.

"I do worry, and I'm not getting any younger. What's going to happen to him after I'm gone?"

"You have a long time before you need to think about that, Sadie. By then, you'll have several grandchildren,"

"Lordy, I hope so."

* * *

Thunder Canyon Ranch...

"This is Thunder Canyon land," Jonas said. "We're about twenty minutes from the house now."

"Why did you name it Thunder Canyon?" Mary Catherine asked.

"Papa named it." Jonas said. "We get some fierce thunderstorms that roar down the valley."

"This is the prettiest place I have ever seen. Of course, I haven't been to many places."

"You traveled across three-fourths of the country," Emma reminded.

"I didn't pay any attention to where we were," Mary Catherine said.

"I love it out here," Emma said. "It's quiet, most of the time."

"When the young'uns are asleep," Jonas said.

"Well, that's true," Emma admitted, "but we don't get many visitors, so I only have Gabby and Pearlie May to talk to besides Wade and the kids.

Wade is our foreman," Emma explained, and Gabby is his wife. Pearlie May is our housekeeper and boss. She's been with Jonas's family forever and runs things around the house."

"That's Wade and Gabby's house over there," Emma said. "Ours is on the right."

"It is beautiful! Mary Catherine exclaimed. "And large. It's as big as the hospital."

"It's home, and it's good to be back. I miss my babies. I'm anxious for you to meet them; come on and I'll introduce you."

Inside...

A large, formidable black woman was in the kitchen. A red scarf was wrapped around her hair, and she wore a large apron to protect her blue dress.

"Pearlie May, this is Mary Catherine," Emma said. "Pearlie May runs the house, so if you need anything, just ask her.

"It's quiet in here; are they taking a nap?"

"Yessum, they plum run me ragged this mornin', and I needed for them to rest so I could git my work done.

"Miss Mary, if you needs anything, you just ast Pearlie May. I believe I hear them chirren stirrin' around up there now."

Mary Catherine's head was on a swivel, trying to take in her surroundings as they climbed the stairs. The house had an air of elegance about it that made her leery of touching anything lest she break it."

Emma looked around a partially open door. "Come give Mama a hug," she said, kneeling. A toddler and a boy that looked to be six or seven immediately ran into her arms.

"I missed you both," she said. "I brought someone home for you to meet.

"Mary Catherine, this little man is Jonas, and this handsome boy is Joshua. Boys, this is Mary Catherine. Can you tell her hello?"

Mary Catherine knelt to be on their level. "I didn't know you had such a big boy. How old are you?" she asked Jonas.

"I'm six-going-on-seven," he said in a sing-song voice. "I'm in second grade and I can read and write."

"Can you read?" she asked Joshua.

"Mama hasn't teached him yet," Jonas said.

Watching the exchange, Emma smiled approvingly. She saw the ease and comfort level of Mary Catherine as she talked to the boys. *She's going to be all right.*

'Let's see if the girls are awake."

One was sitting on the floor playing with a doll. The other was on the bed, rubbing the sleep from her eyes.

"Mama!" she cried. "You're home." She bounded out of bed and into her mother's arms.

"Um, it feels good to hug you. I do believe you've grown since I left. Mary Catherine, this is Lettie. I guess you can figure who she's named for.

"Mattie, aren't you going to give me a hug?"

"Uh huh." She laid her doll down and hugged Emma.

"Girls, this is Mary Catherine. Can you tell her hello and welcome her to our home?"

"Hullo," Mattie said. She immediately turned back to her mother.

"Mama, Jonas has been mean at us."

"How has he been mean to you?" she asked.

"He's been telling us what to do, and wouldn't let us go in the barn. I told him I was going to tell."

"Jonas, have you been trying to boss the girls?"

"They wouldn't do what I told them to do. Papa told them not to go in the barn unless he was there, and I was 'posed to take care of them. They might get hurted."

"He is right, Mattie. There are some dangerous things in the barn."

"Well, he's not the boss of me," Mattie said indignantly."

"What's your doll's name, Mattie?" Mary Catherine asked.

"Angel," Mattie said.

"May I hold her?"

"Uh huh." She handed her the doll.

"She sure is pretty. I've never had a doll."

"You haven't?"

"No, I never did. I always wanted one though."

Mattie went to a box in the corner of the room, and took out a well-worn rag doll, and handed it to Mary Catherine. "You can play with her. I don't play with her anymore."

"What's her name?"

"Name's Miss Betsy."

"Are you sure you don't mind?"

"No, she's old."

"Why don't you show Mary Catherine the blue room. It's going to be her room," Emma said.

Mattie took Mary's hand. "I'll show you." She led her down the hall and opened the door to another room.

Mary Catherine's jaw dropped when she entered. The walls were light blue, with blue curtains. Framed floral prints adorned the walls. The room had a brass bed, with a dresser and a chest of drawers. The dresser had a mirror centered on it.

Her eyes filled with tears. "I've never seen anything like this. I've never even dreamed of anything like it. Miss Emma, it's beautiful."

CHAPTER NINE

The Discussion

"It's one of the saddest things I've ever heard, and at the same time, I was so proud of Mattie I could burst," Emma told Jonas. "She told Mattie she had never had a doll. Mattie got one of her old ones and told her she could play with it. Mary had tears in her eyes. For that matter, so did I."

"What do you think?" he asked. "Will it work?"

"I'm going to make it work," Emma vowed. "I'm going to talk to the kids and see what they think, but they were very much at ease with each other. I would like for her to stay," Emma said. "What do you think, and how much should we pay her?"

"I trust your judgement on staying. My suggestion would be $20 a month starting, and go from there."

"Thank you. I'll talk to her and see what she says."

* * *

She found Mary Catherine sitting on the floor with the two girls, and talking to her doll.

"Mary Catherine, could you come to the parlor for a few minutes? Jonas and I would like to talk to you."

"Yes ma'am. Mattie, will you watch Miss Betsy for me, please?"

"Jonas and I have discussed it, and I have a question for you. I've seen how good you are with the children. Would you like to come stay with us and help me with them?"

"You mean it? You really want me?"

"I mean it. We really want you to stay, and help with all four of them."

She started crying. "I don't believe it," she said. "I can't believe it."

"It's true. We will pay you $20 per month, and of course your room and board are included. The room Mattie showed you will be your room. If it's agreeable, we'll take you to get the rest of your things tomorrow."

Her cheeks flushed. "Miss Emma, I don't have anything else. I brought everything with me."

She missed the quick glance Emma gave Jonas, and his nod in return. "Yes, well, it's all settled then.

You'll need to tell the people at the hospital what you're doing, so they don't worry about you. We'll plan to go into town Wednesday."

Impulsively, Mary Catherine hugged Emma, then apologized. "I shouldn't have done that. I'm sorry."

"It's all right, Mary Catherine. I understand. I don't mean to embarrass you, but you need some clothes,"

"I know. It's one of the reasons I wanted to find paying work. I've never had any money. You didn't embarrass me. I know what my situation is, and I know it isn't my fault."

"When we go to town, we will get some things for you. We will also get some fabric and I will teach you to sew on my sewing machine."

"Miss Emma, I don't know what to say."

"Don't say anything. I have been very fortunate in my life and it's a chance to repay some of it. Just love my children and help me take care of them."

"I will. I promise,"

The next morning...

Pearlie May was already busy at the stove when Mary Catherine entered the kitchen. "Miss Pearlie May, what can I do to help?"

"Chile, first thang is call me Pearlie May. You ain't here to work in my kitchen. This is what I do.

Now Mr. Jonas has already had his first breakfast, and he done already started his work."

"How long have you been here?"

"I been here longer than anyone else. I started when Mr. Jonas was about the baby's age."

"You mean big Mr. Jonas?"

"He the one. They wuz him and Mr. Joshua. He wuz Mr. Jonas's brother. A horse throwed him and broke his neck. Then Miss Olive and Mr. Noah passed. It was a sad time." She looked around. "Thass Miss Emma coming down the stairs."

"Good morning," Emma said. "You're up early. Did you not sleep well?"

"I don't think I even turned over," Mary Catherine said. "The bed is a lot softer than what I've had at the nunnery and the Foundling Home. I'm just used to waking early and helping out, but Miss Pearlie May wouldn't let me."

"She doesn't let me help either," Emma laughed. "The kitchen is hers."

"What time do the children get up?"

"I try to have them up and dressed when Jonas comes back in. He likes to have breakfast with them. You can help me get them dressed, and brush the girl's hair."

"Yes ma'am. Will they be going to town?"

"I don't think so. It's a long trip for Joshua and Lettie."

In town before noon, Jonas asked, "Mary Catherine, do you need to go to the hospital or the nunnery?"

"The nunnery. I would like to talk to the Mother Superior."

"Would you like for me to go with you?" Emma asked.

"Do you mind? I'm a little nervous about it."

"I'll get a haircut while you're there and meet you at the mercantile," Jonas said.

After the meeting, Emma said, "She sounded pleased for you."

"Yes ma'am. She gave me encouragement after I told her what I would like to do, but I think she really wanted me to join the order."

"I can see why. You're a sweet person and good with the children. I would imagine you're just as good with the patients."

"I was really quiet when I first got here. Do you know Mr. Chandler? He's the one I talked to the most. I really liked him."

"Jonas probably knows him. I don't believe we've ever met."

They walked down the street to the mercantile. "Morning, Miss Emma, what brings you back to town so soon?" Silas Farmer asked.

"Good morning, Silas. This is Mary Catherine Esposito. She's helping me with the children.

"Mary, meet Silas Farmer. He owns the mercantile. I guess he's been here as long as anyone in town.

"We just had a few things we needed," she said. "Jonas went to get a haircut and will be meeting us here. In the meantime, we want to look at your ladies' things and then I want to look at some fabrics."

"Help yourself. Let me know if you need any help. I can order anything you want and don't see. Jonas just came in and I need to talk to him."

"Honey, get everything you need while we're here," Jonas said. "It's getting close to roundup, and we're going to be busy. Wade will be getting what he needs.

"What did you want to talk about?" he asked Silas.

Silas motioned with his head and walked over to a corner. "Word is some of Sitting Bull's braves have gone off reservation, and doing some raiding. You might want to keep an eye out."

"I guess I should stock up on ammunition then. We have some, but it wouldn't hurt to have more. Has the Army been involved?"

"I don't think they have yet," Silas said. "So far it's just been running cattle off, stuff like that."

"They've always left us alone. We've always let them have a few head when they need it. I'll let Wade know, so he can be on the lookout. Thanks for the warning though."

CHAPTER TEN

The Lazy J

"Trace, we saw a few Lakota's over in the north section yesterday when we were moving part of the herd to the low pasture," the foreman said.

"How many?"

"We saw three. I don't think they were part of a raiding party. They may have just been young bucks out on their own.

"What do you think we should do, Newt?"

"For now, nothing. They may have just been after a couple of head for food. They didn't do anything, just watched us from the ridgeline. They stayed there though, and they know we saw them. I don't let anybody work alone, and I've already told them to keep a close look out."

"Could we hold them off if they hit us?"

"Depends on how many there were; how many of us are together, and if we have enough ammunition.

I should probably lay in a few more boxes of cartridges. If they hit the house, we could hold them off, but they might try to burn us out. In that case, we'd take our toll, but we might lose the buildings."

"I wonder where the Cavalry is?" Trace said.

"I imagine they are sending out patrols to check out Sitting Bull and make sure he's still on the reservation," Newt replied, "but they can't keep track of small parties like this one."

"I guess we had better make a supply run and get what we need. How many rifles do we have?"

Newt paused. "Everyone has one, and I believe all of them take the 44 cartridge."

"Make up a list, and I'll go in," Trace said. "Include the bunkhouse cook's stuff."

Later...

"Ma, I'm going to town on a supply run," Trace said. "Do you need anything?"

"I do, but I want to go with you. I ain't been off the ranch in two months."

"I don't know if you should, Newt said they saw some Lakota's yesterday when they were moving from the high pasture."

"That don't make no difference," she said. "Besides, I can shoot a Henry as good as you can."

"All right, if you insist, I'm going in tomorrow."

"Maybe we'll run into that Mary Catherine girl."

"Ma..."

"Just saying. It would be nice to see her and Emma again. I'm tired of looking at scruffy cowboy faces."

"Me too."

Silas Farmer Mercantile...

"Silas, I have a list here," Trace said.

"It will be a while before I can get to it," Silas said. "I got the Parson's ahead of you."

"Jonas is here?"

"He was a minute ago. He may have stepped out. His missus is over in the corner."

"Good," Sadie said. "I was hoping we'd run into somebody whilst we were here. I'll go visit with her while we wait."

Emma was holding the dress against Mary Catherine when Sadie found them. "You're Emma Parsons aren't you? I reckon the good Lord was looking out for me. I'm Sadie Jennings from the Lazy J. I didn't expect to see anyone here on a Wednesday. How have you been?"

"Our children have been keeping me busy, but I am getting some help. Do you know Mary Catherine?"

"I sure do. You were at the memorial service for Cort. You were with a sister as I recollect."

"Yes ma'am. It's nice to see you again."

"I was telling Trace just yesterday I was tired of seeing nothing but cowboy faces. You two are a sight for sore eyes. What brings you to town?"

"We needed some things that I had forgotten our last time in. How have you been doing?"

"Tolerable, I guess, but I'm getting along. Summers is good for me and my rheumatism, and I ain't looking forward to winter, but I guess there's nothing I can do about its coming."

"This looks like a good fit," Emma said to Mary Catherine, "add it to the others, and let's look at the fabrics."

"Miss Emma, this is too much," she protested.

"Nonsense, you heard what Jonas said.

"If we're going to be cooped up, we might as well get some sewing done. The way the kids are growing, it's hard to keep up with them," she said to Sadie.

"I remember Trace growing as fast as a weed," Sadie said. "How many do you have?"

"We have four," Emma said. "Two of each."

"I wish Cort and I had been blessed with more. Children need brothers and sisters."

"I agree with you there," Emma said.

"Did you have sisters and brothers?" she asked Mary Catherine.

"I had a lot of them. I grew up in an orphanage."

"Me and my big mouth," Sadie said. "I'm sorry."

"It's all right. It wasn't my fault and I'm not ashamed of it," Mary Catherine said.

"Bless your heart," Sadie said. "I better go keep an eye on Trace to make sure he doesn't miss anything. Y'all going to be in town long?"

"While they get the wagon loaded up, Mary and I are going to visit Lettie," Emma said.

"We're going to have lunch while we're here, and visit with Lettie and Jack," Emma said. "Why don't you and Trace join us?"

"That's kind of you," Sadie said. "but we need to get back home."

Jonas wanted to get home before dark, so their visit with Lettie and Jack was short.

"Well, don't keep me in suspense," Lettie said. "Tell me about it."

"She is darling, and the children love her," Emma whispered. "We came in to tell the sisters she has found a home. We also did some shopping for her. Lettie, she had nothing. I was shocked."

"Miss Lettie, thank you for your help," Mary Catherine said, hugging her tightly. "It's... it's wonderful."

"I'm happy for you," Lettie said. "Emma, thanks."

* * *

"You didn't even talk to her," Sadie said. "You just stood there, like a knot on a log."

"I couldn't think of anything to say, Ma."

"You could have asked how it was to ride the train across the country, or how she likes Montana."

"I didn't think of it."

CHAPTER ELEVEN

Mister Sam

"Mr. Jonas, do you know Mr. Sam Chandler?"

"Yes, I know Sam. He's been around forever. He and Pa were good friends. How do you know him?"

"I got to be friendly with him when he was in the hospital. We talked a lot while he was there."

"What was he in the hospital for?" Jonas asked.

"His horse threw him and he broke his leg badly, but he said that wasn't what happened. He told me, he was still in the saddle when the horse reared and fell on him. He claims he's going to ride it yet. Doctor Palmer told him a man his age has no business trying to... I don't remember what he called it."

"Was it break or bust?"

"Break, that's what the doctor called it," she said.

"Sam must be in his fifties."

"Sixty, the doctor said. He told Sam when you get older your bones get brittle and break easier. Does he have any family?"

"No, he doesn't. His wife passed away some years back and they didn't have any children. He's lived alone since she passed.

"Emma, we should have Sam come for Sunday dinner sometime," Jonas said.

"That's a good idea," she said. "Why don't we send someone over to ask him?"

* * *

"Mighty kind of you to invite me over," Sam said.

"We all wanted to see you, and figured you weren't too busy since Doc told you to take it easy after you broke your leg."

"I was getting kind of restless, sitting there watching the dust settle and the grass grow. Closest thing to excitement I've had."

"Hello, Mr. Sam," Mary Catherine said when she came into the parlor with Lettie on her hip. "Have you been staying away from the horse that broke your leg?"

"You're the onliest one that paid attention when I told you I didn't break my leg, it was that danged horse. What are you doing here?'

"Miss Emma and Mr. Jonas hired me to help with the children. Mr. Sam, this is Lettie. Isn't she sweet? I'm going to put you down, honey, so I can hug Mr. Sam."

"Did you have anything to do with my invite?" he asked.

"It was Mr. Jonas's idea. We were talking about you and he suggested it. I asked him if he knew you.

"First time I ever laid eyes on this boy, he was just a shirttail kid. He was the apple of his mama's eye. This girl is how I kept my senses when I was in the hospital. She would come into my room of a night, and we'd talk till the cows come home. I don't know how she ever got any sleep, she spent so much time in my room. No one else paid any attention to a grumpy old man."

"Now Mr. Sam, you know Sister Anne kept a close eye on you."

"That was because she didn't have anything else to do. Remember I told you something good would happen to you."

"Yes sir, you did, and it came true. I have truly been blessed." Lettie was tugging on Mary's dress and holding her hands up. "Where's Mattie?" Mary

Catherine asked. Lettie pointed upstairs. "Let's go see what's going on. It's pretty quiet. Too quiet with all three of them together."

"I'll see you later, Mr. Sam."

After she left, Sam said, "I really like that girl. She has had a hard life. She told me how it was in the orphanage. There were times when they didn't have enough food to go around, and she went to bed hungry a good many times. I mean to see nothing like that ever happens to her again."

Jonas raised his eyebrows at the last remark. His wife said, "She's a very loving person. The girls love her, and the boys mind her. When we brought her home with us, she literally had only one change of clothes and they were threadbare and didn't fit. Our first order of business was to take care of that. She tried to pay some of it back with her first pay, but of course we wouldn't take it. I'll be back in a few minutes. I want to check with Pearlie May about dinner."

"She's still here?" Sam asked.

"I think she'll be here after I'm in the ground," Jonas said.

"Jonas, did you hear about the Jennings place?"

"No. What happened?"

"It was hit by a raiding party. The main house was burned, but for some reason, they left the barn and the bunkhouse. Trace took a couple of arrows, and Doc Palmer isn't sure he's going to make it. Sadie's staying in town.

"They put up a good fight, and got four or five of them. At least one other hand was hit in the shoulder, but he's going to be all right. Trace was hit twice in the back and shoulder. He's in Saint John's. They were definitely Lakota's. The Army sent a Cavalry patrol after the others. Some people are saying Sitting Bull is going to get the five tribes together. If he does, there will be a war."

"No way he can win a war against the Army," Jonas said, "but I don't blame him for being mad. The white men keep moving in, paying no attention to the treaty and what belongs to the tribes. If Sitting Bull and Crazy Horse get those tribes together, there's going to be hell to pay."

"I hear you, and I agree," Sam said. "In a way, I'm glad I got no women folk to worry about, but Clint Weather's wife is there. I'm going to suggest he send her to town until things settle down."

"I might do the same with Emma and the kids, and Mary Catherine too. That will be a struggle, but maybe she will go because of the kids. I'm glad you told me about this. You butt up against the Lazy J don't you?"

"Some, not all the way down."

"Are you going to move to town?" Jonas asked.

"The good Lord is the only one that's going to make me move off my land," Sam declared.

"I pretty much feel the same way, but I want my family to be safe."

Sam had to return home after dinner. He hugged the ladies and shook hands with Jonas. "Mr. Sam, you be careful, you hear?" Mary Catherine said, hugging him and kissing his cheek."

"Don't you worry none about me," he said. "I'm too ornery to let anything happen to me."

He climbed in his buckboard and drove off. He turned once to look back and waved his hand.

"I didn't know Clint was with him," Jonas said. "I guess he ate with the hands."

"Mr. Sam told me Mr. Weathers and his wife keep pretty close tabs on him."

"That's good to hear," Jonas said.

That evening, after everyone had gone to bed, Jonas told Emma about the Indians seen near the Lazy J. She was shocked at the news. It was the first indication of possible trouble with the Indians since she had come west and she wasn't prepared for it. She was also not prepared for Jonas's request either.

"I want you to take the kids, Mary Catherine, and Pearlie May and stay in town until this is over. We'll take a house so you don't have to stay in the hotel."

"Jonas Parsons, I'm not going off and leave you here. I'm just not going to do it."

"I know you don't want to, but you have to think of the children. We simply can't expose them to that risk."

She lay awake, staring at the ceiling, tears streaming down her cheeks, long after he was asleep.

CHAPTER TWELVE

Out of Nowhere

The day before...

They came out of nowhere, riding their paint ponies bareback, yelling and holding firebrands high. The cowboys of the Lazy J were caught totally by surprise, at the corral. Only one of them was armed.

The firebrands were tossed at the house. One landed on the front porch and another went through an open window.

Trace turned and ran for the house to get his rifle. Arrows make no sound, and he never knew what put him on the ground. A brave jumped from his pony, and straddled Trace on the ground. He had a knife in one hand and a handful of hair in the other, prepared to count coup when Newt came out of the bunkhouse, his rifle in his hand and dropped him with a single shot. He quickly shot another off his pony. The other cowboys had retrieved their handguns and unleashed a fusillade of lead, leaving a total of five Indians on the ground while the others beat a hasty retreat.

Newt had two cowboys along for protection when he took Trace to the hospital in Helena.

The next morning...

Newt sent word to the other ranches.

"I hardly slept last night," Emma said. "I've been thinking about what you said. I don't want to go, but you're right about the children. I guess we have to. I just hope it isn't for too long."

"I'll bring you back just as soon as it's safe."

"You have to promise you'll be careful," she said.

"We've got over twenty hands here," he told her. "Sitting Bull isn't stupid. He will think twice before they come into Thunder Valley, let alone the canyon. We'll go in tomorrow and see how we can work this."

Unsure how long it might take to find a suitable house, Jonas went to the hotel first. "I need four rooms," he told the desk clerk."

"Yes sir. How long will you be needing them?" the clerk asked.

"I don't rightly know at this time," Jonas said.

"We can accommodate you, sir," the clerk replied and gave him four keys.

Pearlie May was behind Mary Catherine, carrying two of the valises. "Sir... Mr. Parsons, may I speak with you please?" the clerk asked.

"Yes, what is it?" Jonas asked.

"You didn't plan on her staying here, did you?" he asked, indicating Pearlie May.

"Yes, I do. She is part of my family."

"Sir, they aren't allowed in the hotel."

"By whose rule?"

"It's the policy of the hotel," the unctuous clerk said.

"Is Gabe Hartley here?" Jonas asked, his voice as cold as the inside of a stone crypt.

"Yes sir," the clerk said.

"Get him," Jonas commanded.

The clerk hurried away and returned with a rotund man, wearing a coatless suit. "What is the problem," he asked.

"Your employee said my housekeeper is not allowed to stay here."

"That is the policy of the hotel," Hartley said. No Indians, Chinese or other persons of color."

"Do you have any idea how much business I've done over the years with your hotel and restaurant."

"Not exactly," Hartley said, "But probably considerable."

"I would say considerable is correct. I am trying to keep my family safe, if you can't accommodate us, all of us, you will never get another dime of my money."

"Let's not be hasty, Jonas. You understand how it is. The other guests would not like it."

"I saw a lot of keys in the slots. Just how many other guests do you have at the present time?"

"Well, I can't say off the top of my head, but there are some."

Jonas spun on his heels. "Emma, y'all go over to Jack and Lettie's while I see what I can do."

She could tell by his face, he was angry. Angrier than she had ever seen. "What's the problem?"

"I'll tell you later," he said.

"Jonas... Mr. Parsons, I will bend the rule for you. I can see this is of some concern to you. Out of deference to the other guests, I would like for her to remain out of the view of our other guests. It will be all right if she uses the rear door."

"Hartley, Pearlie May has been a part of the Parsons family longer than I have. I can assure you I am not going to forget this."

Jonas went to the bank and asked for the owner. "Jonas, what can I do for you?" Charles Waters asked.

"Charley, There's been some Indian activity, and I want to have the family stay in town until it's passed. Hartley doesn't want to put us up at the hotel because Pearlie May is with us. Does the bank have anything that we can use until this dies down?"

"I do have a house empty, It isn't anything grand, but it's not a shanty. It's probably better than the hotel, but it will take a bit of cleaning since it's been empty for a while. Are you going to be staying in town too?"

"No, it will be Emma, the kids, Mary Catherine and Pearlie May. I'll be going back to the ranch after they're settled in. I imagine the Army will put this thing down pretty quickly."

"I heard about the Jennings place. Has there been any other?"

"Not that I've heard about. I just don't want to have them in danger if it isn't necessary."

"Let me get my hat and I'll show you the house."

"I want Emma to see it too. She went to the parsonage while I got this settled."

"We'll stop by and get her," the banker said.

On the way, Jonas said, "You know, it's been playing in my head for a while, it might be a good idea to get a place to stay in town. We could use it instead of the hotel, and it might come in handy in the winter."

When Jonas told Emma about the hotel problem, she was irate. "Pearlie May is a lot cleaner and nicer than the cowboys and miners that stay there. I'm glad you did what you did."

"I told him she's been a member of the Parsons family longer than I have. Charley Waters has a house we can use if it's okay with you."

"I'm sure it will be fine," Emma said.

"Let's go look anyway."

The house was dusty, but serviceable. "We can get whatever we need from Silas," Jonas said. "Charley, this will do fine. I'd like to rent it, name your price. I'll just keep it for a while."

"Thank you, Mr. Waters," Emma said. "We appreciate it."

Two days later, Pearlie May, Mary Catherine and Emma had the place cleaned up and stocked. "I'll go back to the ranch tomorrow," Jonas said.

"That's the part I'm not looking forward to," Emma said.

"Nor am I, but I will be back and forth," Jonas promised.

"Won't that be dangerous?" Emma asked.

"I won't come alone," he said.

"I would rather you not do that," she said. "I will miss you and so will the kids, but just come take us home as soon as possible."

"I will."

CHAPTER THIRTEEN

Visiting

"Do you think it would be all right if I go by the hospital and see how Trace Jennings is doing?" Mary Catherine asked.

"Of course it would," Emma said. "Would you mind if I go with you?"

"Not at all. I've only met him the one time at the memorial service they had. Sister Anne and I went, and Miss Lettie introduced us to him and his mother."

After they determined where he was, Mary Catherine led the way. "I guess you learned the layout pretty well," Emma said.

"Yes ma'am. I've been in every corner, and cleaned most of them." They met Sister Anne in the hall.

"I'm glad we ran into you," Mary Catherine said. "I was going to look you up before we left. Sister

Anne, this is Mrs. Emma Parsons. Miss Emma, Sister Anne was very kind and helped me while I was here."

"You are looking well," Sister Anne said. "I've been wondering how you were doing."

"I am doing well. Miss Emma and Mr. Jonas are wonderful to work for, and I love their children."

"They love you right back too," Emma said. "We've come to see the Jennings boy. Mr. Chandler told us what happened and how serious it was. How is he doing?"

"Not very well, I'm afraid," Sister Anne replied. "Doctor Palmer has operated on him twice now, and we're just not sure of the outcome."

"Is Mrs. Jennings here?" Emma asked.

"She doesn't leave," Sister Anne said. "I'm afraid she is going to make herself ill if she doesn't take better care of herself. Do you know her?"

"Not very well, but my husband does. We just heard what happened to her son. Jonas knew her husband quite well. Mary Catherine told me about him."

"How is that dear Mr. Chandler? We haven't seen him since he was discharged."

"He seems to be doing well," Mary Catherine said. "Miss Emma and Mr. Jonas invited him to dinner last week. I asked if he had done anything to the horse, and he said his foreman won't let him anywhere near him. It was good to see him again. I really like him."

"The Jennings boy is in a room down the hall."

"We stopped at the desk and asked," Emma said. "It's nice to meet you Sister. Mary has told us about you."

"She is a dear child, and I'm pleased she is doing well."

"We think a lot of her too."

In the room...

"We were shocked to hear about your son," Emma said. "When we heard what happened, Jonas packed us up and moved us into town until the trouble has passed. We've rented a house down from the church. We would like for you to have dinner with us.

"I can't leave Trace," Sadie said. "He's all I have left, and now there's a good chance I'll lose him too."

"Is he asleep?" Mary Catherine asked.

"Doctor Palmer is keeping him this way, hoping it will help him heal. The chest is what's real bad. The shoulder has already got well, but the other one tore things up pretty bad."

"Mrs. Jennings, you look exhausted. Have you had any sleep?" Mary Catherine asked,

"Just what I can get in the chair. I have to be here in case..." She didn't elaborate. Her meaning was clear.

"I'll stay with him while you rest," Mary Catherine said. "How long since you've had anything to eat?"

"I haven't felt like eating. I got to be here all the time," she said.

"You come with me," Emma said. "Mary Catherine will stay with Trace."

"I can't. I..."

"I won't take no for an answer. Now come along. Trace wouldn't want you to wind up getting sick from worrying about him. You need to eat to keep your strength up."

"You know she's right," Mary Catherine said. "Now you go with her. I won't leave the room until you get back, and if anything happens, I'll get Sister Anne, and then I'll come after you. Just tell me where you'll be."

Ten hours later, an embarrassed Sadie reentered the room. "I'm so sorry to leave you that long," she said. "Emma took me to her house, and after I ate, I lay across the bed for just a minute, and didn't wake up for nine hours."

"Miss Pearlie May's cooking has put me to sleep more than once," Mary Catherine said. "I didn't mind staying at all. I had the chance to talk to Sister Anne for a while. Doctor Palmer came in and said he's holding on, so I guess that's good news. Other than that, I don't have anything to tell you."

"Why are you doing this?" Sadie asked.

"I've been given so much since I got here, that I want to give something back. The Lord has blessed me with a good job, and the Parsons have been good to me."

"When we saw you at the memorial for my husband, you said you came here on the mercy train. I never heard of it before."

"The Foundling Home in New York City, where I was, takes in so many orphans they don't have room for them. They send forty or fifty out at a time, along with three or four sisters to take care of them, hoping to get the children adopted. I wasn't, so the sisters let me stay in the nunnery and help out here. Miss Lettie introduced me to Miss Emma and Mr. Jonas, and they offered me a job helping Miss Emma. I'm very blessed."

"How did you lose your parents, if you don't mind me asking."

"I don't know if I did. I was left on the steps at the convent when I was about two months old. They took me in, but I was never adopted. I was getting too old to stay there, so I asked if I could go on the train."

"That is so sad. Sometimes I don't understand the Lord's ways. Cort and I wanted more children, and now I don't even have him, and they have so many back there they have to send them out on trains. It just don't make no sense."

"The sisters told me the mothers love their babies so much and know they can't take care of them, so they leave them where they can be helped. I like to believe it's true."

"It takes a strong person to go through all that and still come out kind and loving."

"Thank you Mrs. Jennings. I appreciate it. Now I had better go see what I can do to help at home."

"God bless you, Mary Catherine. You're a good person."

"I'll be back later and let you get out again."

Sadie sat by her son's bed and took his hand. "Son, the most wonderful girl I ever met just left. I hope she comes back again. I hope you're awake to meet her."

CHAPTER FOURTEEN

The Hospital

The fourth time Mary Catherine went to the hospital was in the evening. "You go use my bed, and I'll stay," she told Sadie. "A night's rest and a good hot breakfast will be good for you. Now go. Miss Emma's expecting you."

"Are you sure?"

"I wouldn't have offered if I wasn't sure," she said.

The hospital lights had been dimmed and it was quiet. The sister on duty came in to take a look. Satisfied, she went on to the next room.

Mary Catherine heard a sound and went to the bedside. Trace was moving his head from side to side, wild eyed. She took his hand. "It's all right, you're in the hospital."

"Mama?" he croaked.

"Your mother went to get some rest. Let me get you a sip of water." She put her hand behind his head and lifted it slightly. She held the glass to his dry, parched lips. Easy, just a sip for now. I'll hold the glass." She pulled the glass back, "Not too fast, it might make you choke and we don't want that to happen. One more sip. There, that's enough for now."

She lowered his head to the pillow. "I'm going to let the sister know you woke up. I'll be right back."

She found Sister Elizabeth in the ward. "Sister, Mr. Jennings was awake. He tried to speak, and his lips were dry, so I gave him two sips of water, and I think he's gone back to sleep."

"You should not have given him anything without me being present."

"Sister Elizabeth. It's Mary Catherine. Don't you remember me? I worked here a lot of nights. I knew what to look for."

"I didn't recognize you," she said. "These old eyes don't work in the dark as well as they once did. Why are you here?"

"We are staying in town until the Indian scare is over. I came to let Mrs. Jennings get some rest. She looked worn out."

"Bless you child. She needed it, and no one could convince her it was best."

"She'll be back in the morning," Mary Catherine told her. "I should have let you know I was here, but I had promised Mrs. Jennings I wouldn't leave him. I want to get back in there if it's all right with you."

"You go ahead. I'll be in when I finish in here."

Back in the room, she found Trace still moving and waving his arm. Unsure whether he might hurt himself, she took the hand that was waving into both of hers and began rubbing the back with her thumb, talking softly. He calmed, stopped waving and went back to sleep.

When the sister came in, Mary Catherine told her what happened. "I wasn't sure whether he would hurt himself so I calmed him down, and he went back to sleep."

"How did you do that?" the curious sister Elizabeth asked.

"I held his hand and talked to him quietly. Sister Anne told me about it."

"Good for you. You would do well in this."

"I am already blessed to have a job I dearly love, and I think I'm good at."

"Any time you would like, come back, we always appreciate the help."

"It would be wrong of me to accept pay from Mr. Parsons and then not do the work."

"Are you going to be here the rest of the night?" the sister asked.

"I will be here until Mrs. Jennings comes back."

The next morning...

Mrs. Jennings hugged Mary Catherine when she walked in and looked at her sleeping son. "Any changes?" she asked hopefully.

Mary Catherine smiled. "Actually, he woke twice during the night. He asked for you the first time. I gave him some water, and he went back to sleep. Then he woke again briefly. When Doctor Palmer comes in, be sure to tell him about it, and if he has any questions, ask Sister Elizabeth. I asked her to come in and check. Did you sleep?"

"I sure did. You've been a godsend. I don't know if I could have made it much longer without your help."

"You would have done what you had to do. You're a strong woman."

"God bless you, Mary Catherine."

* * *

"Sister gave me some good news," Dr. Palmer said when he made his rounds.

"He's awakened several times," Sadie said. "He's talked a little, but his voice is scratchy."

"Each time he awakens, give him water, but don't let him gulp it down."

He removed the dressings. "It looks good. I don't see any sign of infection, which is always one thing to worry about. Maybe the last surgery took care of everything. I've ordered a lesser amount of medication, so he should be awake more, and also more alert. I don't think I'm being overly optimistic when I say he is probably going to be all right, barring any unanticipated developments.

"I'm worried about you though. Have you been eating and getting rest?"

"For the past two or three days or maybe four, Mary Catherine has been staying, and I've stayed with Emma Parsons. They've taken a house in town until the Indian trouble dies down. It has been a blessing for me."

"Mary Catherine is good. She learned a lot when she was here in the hospital, and has turned out to be an effective nurse's aide."

"Is she coming today?" Trace asked.

"I don't know," Sadie said. "Now you're better, I don't need to stay here all the time, and I can quit imposing on them."

"I doubt they see it that way," Dr. Palmer said. "Sister will put a clean dressing on, while I get on with my rounds. I think you're out of the woods. By the way, I have a present for you." He reached into his pocket and withdrew two arrow heads. I have another patient a while back who dated and framed the arrow I took out of his chest. It hangs on their wall."

"I don't want to touch them," Sadie said. "They almost killed him."

"I want to keep them," Trace said. "Did we lose anyone?"

"Two others were hit, but nowhere near as bad as you," Sadie said. "They're back at home. Part of the front of the house was burned, and they've already started fixing it."

"What about the Indians?" he asked.

"Five were killed. The Army went after the others. I haven't heard any more about it since I came in with you."

"How long am I going to have to stay here?" he asked.

"Until the doctor says you're okay. Until yesterday, we didn't even know whether you were going to make it or not."

CHAPTER FIFTEEN

Quiet

That same afternoon...

Mary Catherine entered Trace's room to find him sitting up and propped on a pillow. "Where's your mother?" she asked.

"She went to the mercantile to get a few things, and to the hotel," he replied. "She told me you've been here a lot. Why?"

"She needed help. She was exhausted, and wasn't eating or doing anything else. Miss Emma and the sisters convinced her she was going to make herself sick and wouldn't do you any good, so I spelled her. She didn't ask for help if that's what you wanted to know."

"I just wondered why you did it, since we don't know you or anything."

"Why were you in town?"

"When Mr. Jonas heard what happened, he got a house here in town and moved all of us here until he thinks it's safe to go back home."

"Home? You live there?"

"Not that it's any of your business, but I work for them helping with the children. I'm not sure why all your questions."

"I just want to know what's going on," he said.

"What's going on is, I was helping your mother. I'm sorry it bothers you accepting help. Now you are better, and there is no reason for me to be here any longer. Goodbye, and I won't trouble you again. I'll leave a note for your mother."

She borrowed a pencil and wrote a short note to Mrs. Jennings and left it on the chair.

* * *

"Mary Catherine was here?" Sadie asked.

"She came in right after you left," he replied. "She left a note."

Sadie read the note. "What did you say to her?"

"She just asked where you were, and I told her. I asked why she had been here so much and she said you needed help. I asked her why she was in town and she told me it was because of the raid on us. She told me she was working for them. She wondered about why I was asking the questions, and I said I just wanted to know what was going on. That's when she said she would leave you a note. What did she say we talked about?"

"She just said she was glad you were better and was glad she could help. I think you must have hurt her feelings."

"Ma, I didn't say anything to hurt her feelings, I told you what we talked about and that was it."

* * *

"I didn't expect you back so soon," Emma said.

"He's better, and they don't need me anymore," Mary Catherine said. "Do you have any idea when we're going home?"

"No, but I expect Jonas to come in the next day or so. Maybe he will have an idea.

It was three days before Jonas appeared, After a reunion with his children, he told Emma he was waiting to hear from the Cavalry Lieutenant leading the patrol, and didn't know when that would be. He stayed another three days before returning to the ranch.

Ten days passed before the patrol reappeared. "We caught up with the ones that raided the Lazy J," the Lieutenant told Jonas. "It was what we thought.

They were young bucks that had gone off the reservation. Sitting Bull has moved the tribe to another area, and there shouldn't be any more trouble around here."

"That's good news, Lieutenant. I can bring my family back home."

It was late in the day, so he waited until the next morning to head for town.

"Who wants to go for a ride?" he asked.

"Where to?" his son asked.

"I thought we might go home. How does that sound?"

"Good. When will we leave?"

"As soon as we get packed up," he said. "Wade is at the mercantile loading supplies and some grain, but we don't have to wait for him."

Two hours later, they were home. "It sure feels good to be home. I hope we never have to do something like that again," Emma said. "I didn't like being separated."

* * *

The day after they left, Sadie went to the house the Parsons family had rented. She wanted to find out what had transpired between Mary Catherine and Trace. There was no answer to her knock. *I guess they've gone home. I wanted to thank them for their help*. Back in the hospital, she told Trace how disappointed she was.

"Ma, I told you what happened," he said. "It wasn't a big thing."

"I wanted to thank them. I slept in their house, and ate their food. Mary Catherine spent three whole nights sitting in here just so I would get some rest. If you died, I didn't want you to be alone. We owe them, especially her."

Doctor Palmer released Trace with directions to take it easy for two more weeks, and to return for a follow-up check. "Don't catch any more arrows," he said. "An inch to the right and you wouldn't have survived."

Trace blanched. He hadn't realized how close to death he had come. "I didn't realize it was that bad," he said.

CHAPTER SIXTEEN

A Meeting

Two months later...

"Emma!" Sadie said. "What luck running into you today. I went to where you were staying to thank you for your kindness while Trace was in the hospital, but you had already left."

"It was nothing," Emma said. "You would have done the same for us if the situation had been reversed."

"It was something, and I appreciate it. Is that darling Mary Catherine still staying with you?"

"She is a nanny for the children and lives with us, if that's what you mean."

"I didn't realize she worked for you," Sadie said.

"She has really become one of our family. She has made things much easier for me."

"Has she said anything to you about what happened at the hospital?"

"I don't know what you mean," Emma said.

"I think Trace said something that hurt her feelings. She left a note for me and we didn't see her again."

"She hasn't said anything to me, but it wouldn't be like her to say anything. I've never heard her say an unkind word about anyone."

"Is she with you?"

"She's with the children. We're still renting the house to use when we come to town. We're not going back until after church tomorrow. Would you like to get together? I'd love to hear how your house is progressing."

"We're staying at the hotel tonight. Want to meet there for dinner?"

Emma smiled ruefully and shook her head. "When we were looking for a place during the Indian scare, Jonas was going to take four rooms for us. Then the clerk said Pearlie May couldn't stay there. Jonas told them they would never get another dime of his money, and he meant it. What about the cafe?"

"The cafe is fine," Sadie said. "Six o'clock?"

"We'll see you then," Emma said.

Back at the house...

"I saw Sadie Jennings today," Emma said. "She and Trace are staying at the hotel. I told her we would meet them at the cafe for dinner. I'm anxious to hear about their house."

"Miss Emma, I would rather not go, if it's all right with you."

"Is there a problem?" Emma asked.

"I just wouldn't be comfortable being there."

"I certainly don't want to do anything that makes you uncomfortable. Sadie will be disappointed. She wanted to thank you for helping her when Trace was in the hospital."

"I didn't do anything any other person wouldn't have done."

"I'm not sure I agree with you on that point."

"I'll fix dinner for the children and you and Mr. Jonas can enjoy the evening with your friends."

"They're acquaintances. I hadn't met her before I saw her at the hospital. Jonas knew her husband, but that's it."

"Thank you Miss Emma, I'm glad you understand."

The Cafe...

"Mary Catherine didn't come?" Sadie asked.

She's staying with the children," Emma said.

"Oh, we did so want to see her," Sadie said. "Are you going to be at church tomorrow?"

"We plan to go, and then go home after services."

"We'll see her then," Sadie said.

"I'm not sure whether she will be there. I don't know how comfortable she is about going to a Protestant church," Emma said. "She's always gone to the Catholic Church."

Later...

"Mary Catherine, we're going to church tomorrow before going home. Will you be going with us?" Emma asked.

"Yes ma'am, if it's all right with you. I would like to see Miss Lettie."

"Good. I can use your help keeping the kids reined in."

"They won't be any trouble. They've been good all evening."

"Now that scares me. They're saving their energy for tomorrow. Maybe we can rip a pillow cover or something and gag them."

After breakfast, Emma and Mary Catherine got dressed and then helped the children with their clothes.

"Feel the difference in the air?" Jonas asked. "Fall is here. I can smell it. It won't be long before we see snow on the peaks."

"It will be exciting for me to see snow," Mary Catherine said. "In the orphanage, we weren't allowed to go out in it."

"You will get your fill of it and then some here," Jonas said. "It will be waist deep between the house and the barn. We will have ropes tied between the buildings as lifelines. When it freezes, we have to go out to the creeks and punch through the ice so the cattle can drink. If it is really deep, we'll have to haul hay out to them."

"Can't they break through the ice?" she asked.

"They could if they weren't so stupid," he said. "Cattle are the dumbest creatures on this earth."

She laughed. "That's funny."

"It's not funny when you're out in it swinging an axe," he said.

"I didn't know you were serious."

"A cowboy's life is dangerous. He's out in all kinds of weather, thunderstorms and blizzards alike. You'll see."

"You should hear some of the stories about stampedes," Emma said. "They go out in the worst of it. When I first got here, I couldn't believe it.

Now, I just pray everything will be okay, and he'll come home when it's over."

"You don't have to go out in it, do you?" Mary Catherine asked.

"I don't ask them to do anything I won't do. It wouldn't be fair," he said.

She looked at Emma, who simply nodded her head. "It's one reason they respect him. He gets dirty and freezes right alongside them, just as he did when he sent us to town because of the raiding."

"Papa was the same way," Jonas said. "In fact, every rancher I've ever known is that way."

"That's how Mr. Sam broke his leg," Mary Catherine said. "Oh. I forgot. He didn't break it. That danged horse did it." Emma and Jonas laughed.

"Is that what he said?" Jonas asked.

"It's what he told Sister Anne and Miss Lettie. I wonder if he'll be there?"

"Probably," Jonas said.

"I hope so. He's one of my favorite people."

Trace and Sadie were sitting near the front when the Parsons family entered. There was not enough room in the same pew, so they sat in the row behind them. It was early, so they had time to chat.

Sam Chandler stood at the end of their seat. "Room for an old man?" he asked.

"Always room for you, Mr. Sam," Mary Catherine said, moving the small Lettie from the seat and holding her on her lap. Joshua was on his mother's lap and everyone was effectively separated.

"How are you doing," Sam asked. "They treating you all right?"

"Yes sir, I couldn't ask for it to be any better."

"Jonas, I've been looking at the woolly caterpillars. They're telling me it's going to be a hard winter."

"Papa used to take notice of them too," Jonas said. "I never could tell anything by them, but he set great store in what he saw. I had better lay in some extra hay."

"I'm doing that too," Sam said. "I'll be all set if it's in short supply." He looked at Mary Catherine. "You're thinking we're crazy aren't you? What you look at is how thick their coat is. If it's thick there's gonna be cold and lots of snow. I'm telling you true."

Lettie Owens went to the piano and began playing the introit as the choir moved to their places. Jack raised his hands above his head and said, "Let us pray." A hush fell over the congregation as he prayed.

CHAPTER SEVENTEEN

I Told You So

After the service, Sadie approached Mary Catherine. "I was hoping to see you last night," she said.

"I was taking care of the children," Mary Catherine said.

"I want to know what my boy did that upset you," Sadie said.

"He didn't do anything, Mrs. Jennings. He was better, so I went back to doing what I'm paid to do, the same as I was doing last night."

"You work for them?"

"Yes ma'am. I do."

"Well, that may be so, but I still want to know what happened."

"It is the truth. He was better, and there was no need for anyone to sit there all night."

"I just wanted to thank you for what you did. I would like to pay you."

"No ma'am. You're a neighbor, and you were in need. I'm glad I was able to help. If you'll excuse me, I need to take Joshua off Miss Emma's hands."

"I don't believe that girl," Sadie said.

"You should believe her," Lettie Owens overheard the remark. "She is the real thing."

"I wish she'd take kindly toward my Trace. He needs someone like her."

"He should speak for himself," Lettie said.

"He should," Sadie said, "and I've told him, but he gets all tongue tied when he's around her and looks anywhere except at her. He ain't nothing like Cort was. Cort never met a stranger."

"That's one disadvantage of living on a ranch or farm. You don't have as many people to interact with. I'd lose my senses if I didn't have contact with people."

"You have a way about you that just naturally attracts people," Sadie said.

"I take that as a compliment, thank you," Lettie said.

"Do you have any suggestions?"

"The only thing I have is to get involved with others."

"I tried that, by asking them to dinner, but Mary Catherine didn't come, she stayed with the children. I actually confronted her about it. That's what you overheard."

"My take on that is she sees herself as an employee and not a member of the family and feels a sense of responsibility about doing what she is paid to do. Emma gave her a lifeline and she doesn't want to lose it. Remember, I don't know if she's even eighteen yet."

"She seems older," Sadie said.

"Life made her that way. She's been through a lot."

Thunder Canyon Ranch...

"Is something wrong?" Emma asked.

"Mrs. Jennings is upset with me because I wasn't with you at the cafe. She didn't believe me when I told her Trace hadn't said or done anything to make me mad. I told her twice he was better and didn't need to have someone stay in the room all night. I told her I needed to get back to the job I'm being paid to do. I said it was what I was doing the night of the dinner."

"I think I know what this is about," Emma said. "You have just run into a matchmaking mother."

"I don't know what you mean."

"She has an unmarried son, you are an unmarried girl she thinks would make a good wife for her son. She's frustrated that her attempts to get you two together are not working."

"I am flabbergasted. I have never given any thought to marriage to anyone. I'm not old enough to get married. I am just barely eighteen."

"Out here, it's not uncommon for sixteen and seventeen year olds to marry. I personally think it is too young, but it happens. A girl in her twenties is considered an old maid if she isn't married.

"The second thing that bothers me, is your attitude toward yourself and us. We consider you to be part of our family, while you seem to think you're just a person hired to help. I want you to think about something. You saw what Jonas did when the hotel wouldn't let Pearlie May in the hotel or wanted to keep her out of sight. He told them she's been a part of the Parsons family longer than he has. Except for the time part of it, we feel the same about you."

"If I'm part of the family, then I shouldn't be paid for helping."

"Pearlie May gets paid. I have access to anything I want, so I'm being paid in a manner of speaking. We're both part of the family. You never had a family before, but you do now. Being a member of the family carries responsibilities, for you, me,

Pearlie May and even the children. Jonas has the biggest responsibility of any of us because he is responsible for taking care of us and providing for us. It's what he was doing when he had us move to town."

"I need to sit down," Mary Catherine said. "This is a lot for me to take in all at once."

"I meant every word I said," Emma told her.

* * *

"Jonas, I've been thinking about Mary Catherine."

"What about her?"

"I would like to adopt her. I think we should have done it from the get go."

"I'm not objecting, but what brought this on?" he asked.

"Sadie has been trying to play matchmaker between Mary Catherine and Trace. It's why the dinner the other night. She confronted her about why she didn't come. Mary told her she was being paid to do a job and that's what she was doing. She said Sadie didn't believe her. She might be eighteen in age, but in her mind, she's nowhere near ready to even consider being married and I agree with her."

"How do you think she would feel about it?"

"I'm sure she would be surprised, and I think she would be thrilled. I told her she's a part of the family, the same as Pearlie May is a part. She countered by saying if she's a member, then she shouldn't be paid for helping."

"Does she know Pearlie May is paid?"

"She does now. I also told her I had access to anything I need or want, so in a sense, I am being paid too."

"Let's talk to her and see how she feels," he said.

"I knew you'd feel that way." She kissed him. "Not that you need luck, but you're going to get lucky tonight."

The children had been read to and were all in bed. "Mary Catherine, Jonas and I would like to talk to you before you go to bed."

CHAPTER EIGHTEEN

A Dream Come True

An apprehensive Mary Catherine sat on the davenport facing Emma and Jonas.

"We want to talk about your role here, and we want to correct a mistake we made when we first met you," Jonas said.

Worried now, Mary Catherine said "Y... yes sir?"

"Emma and I had a long talk, and came to a decision. How would you like to become our daughter?"

Her jaw dropped. "You mean..."

"We would like to become your parents and adopt you. Because of your age, it would have to be with your permission."

Her hands went to her face and she began crying "You really mean it?" she asked between sobs.

"We really mean it," Emma said. "If it's all right with you, we'll see our attorney and make all of the arrangements. I imagine we will have to go before a judge who will ask you questions and all. We would like to do it as soon as possible."

"No one ever wanted me before. I can't believe I'm going to have a family."

"Dear, you've had a family since you came to us," Emma said, gently.

"I feel like running and yelling so everyone will know I'm not an orphan anymore."

"You just go right ahead and do that. We'll be going back to town in the next day or so to get this taken care of."

* * *

The papers were prepared and signed. Judge Horner, his spectacles perched on his nose, looked over the document. He laid it on his desk and peered at Mary Catherine over the tip of his glasses. "Is this something you want?"

"Yes sir. It's what I've wanted ever since I realized I had no family. I want it more than I can tell you with words."

"One last question. Your name, Esposito, do you want to keep it or do you want it to be Parsons?"

"Sir, the Sisters gave me Esposito, It would be the best thing in the world for me if I can be a Parsons."

"So ordered, Mary Catherine, you are now the legally adopted daughter of Jonas and Emma Parsons."

"Thank you, thank you, thank you," she said.

"Does this mean I can call you Mama and Papa?" she asked.

"It does," Jonas said. "Now hug your Papa."

It was a fierce hug.

"Miss Emma, thank you too," she said, wrapping her arms around Emma's neck and sobbing on her shoulder.

"I'm not Miss Emma, I'm Mama or Mother."

"Yes ma'am, I mean yes, Mama. This is the best day of my entire life," she said. "I have sisters, brothers and parents. All of the things I've ever wanted."

Emma nudged Jonas. "We've made one person in the world happy today. She deserves it too."

"I think you're right."

That Sunday, the Christian Church...

"I have an announcement to make," Jack Owens said from the pulpit. "We have a new member in our church family. I ask you all to make welcome Miss Mary Catherine Parsons. Mary Catherine, would you stand please, so everyone will recognize you, and welcome you to the church family?"

A beaming Mary Catherine stood and faced the congregation. She didn't bother to wipe away the tears running down her cheeks. She reached down and tugged Emma to her feet. Emma put her arm around her. Mother and daughter stood together as the congregation applauded.

After services, the Parsons were approached by many offering their congratulations and welcome. Mary Catherine later told Emma, "That made me feel warm and a part of everything."

"That's why Jack does that with visitors and new members," Emma replied. "I was embarrassed when I first came here and he did it."

"I'm happy for you, Mary Catherine," Sadie Jennings said.

"So am I," Trace said. "I don't think I ever thanked you properly for what you did, but I do appreciate it. So does Mama."

"You're welcome," Mary Catherine said. "I'm glad I was able to help."

"Are y'all staying for the picnic?" Trace asked.

"We are. Mama brought a large basket of food," Mary Catherine said.

"There's always plenty to eat. When I was little, Ma used to get on me because all I would get was cake and pie. She started fixing my plate and only put one dessert on the plate."

"Does she still do that?"

"I'm allowed to do my own now, but she watches what I get. Would it be all right if I sat with you?"

Surprised, she hesitated before answering. "I guess it will be all right."

"Good." He started to say something else but was interrupted by Sam Chandler.

"My favorite girl has a family!" Sam Chandler said. "I would have adopted you, but folks would have talked about me being a dirty old man."

"Mr. Sam, I haven't been here all that long, but I've never heard anyone say anything but the best about you. I'm pleased to be your friend."

"God bless you. You bring a joy to this old man. I just wish my wife could have known you. We'd have adopted you for sure."

"That's one of the nicest things anyone has ever said to me. Thank you, Mr. Sam."

"I'll see you later, Mary Catherine," Trace said.

"Everyone is being so nice to me. They make me feel like I belong."

"You do belong," Emma said. "I found the same thing. I guess it's because of the hard life on the edge. They're always ready to help, before you even ask. You fit right in with everyone."

CHAPTER NINETEEN

Sadness

Two years later...

"What's wrong, honey," Emma asked when Jonas came in after all day in the saddle. "Tired?".

"Sam Chandler died in his sleep last night."

"Oh no," she said.

"I ran into Clint Weathers, and he told me they found him this morning after he didn't come for breakfast."

"This is really going to hurt Mary Catherine," Emma said. "He has been one of her favorite people ever since she got here. I don't suppose they know when the funeral will be?"

"It will probably be this Sunday. Clint said he will be buried next to his wife on the ranch. Do you want me to tell Mary Catherine, or would you rather do it?"

"I will," Emma said. "They went for a walk."

The girls were red faced when they returned, so Pearlie May fixed lemonade for them.

Emma found them on the front porch. "Girls go inside. I need to talk to your sister," she said.

"What is it, Mama?"

"Jonas got some bad news today. Mr. Sam died in his sleep last night. When he didn't come for breakfast, Mrs. Weathers found him in his bed this morning."

The reaction was immediate. Mary Catherine burst into tears. Emma embraced her. "I know how much you liked him," she said.

"He told me last Sunday he hadn't been feeling well and had seen Dr. Palmer," Mary Catherine said. I didn't expect this. When is the funeral?"

"It's not set yet, but Jonas thinks it will be this Sunday. We'll go of course."

"Thank you, Mama. I'm going to miss him. He was the first person I knew who wasn't connected to the Church."

The funeral was held at the Circle C Ranch, beneath the trees where Sam's wife had been laid to rest. Sam had known everyone in the county and was well liked by all. Most of them turned out for the service conducted by Jack Owens. Mary Catherine cried the entire time. A somber Trace Jennings tried to comfort her, not knowing what to say. She leaned her head on his shoulder, sobbing.

Wednesday...

A buggy stopped in front of the ranch house. "Hello the house," the driver called. "Hello the house."

Jonas was at the corral and heard the call. He jumped off the fence and walked to the front. "I'm Jonas Parsons. What can I do for you?"

"I'm Phineas Tolliver, attorney at law. I am here to see a Miss..." He adjusted his spectacles and took a paper from his inside coat pocket. "Miss Mary Catherine Esposito."

"Parsons. Her name is Mary Catherine Parsons now."

"Yes, I have business with her. Is she available?"

"I'm her father. What does this business involve?"

"My paper indicates she is an orphan," the lawyer said.

"Was an orphan. We legally adopted her two years ago. If you want to talk to my daughter, you will have to tell me what it's about."

"She was named a beneficiary in a will," Tolliver said.

"Sam Chandler's will?"

"You know Mr. Chandler?"

"All my life. His ranch butts up against mine. Come inside and I'll get Mary Catherine."

"If you wait in the parlor, she'll be with you in a minute. Can I get you anything? Tea, water?"

"Water would be good. It's a long drive from Helena."

Jonas went to the kitchen. "Pearlie May, Is Mary Catherine upstairs?"

"She in the girls bedroom."

"Would you get Mr. Tolliver some water please? I'll get her."

She was sitting on the floor with Mattie and Lettie. "Mary Catherine, there is someone here to see you."

The puzzled look on her face spoke volumes. Jonas said, "He's a lawyer and needs to talk to you. I will be in the room, and you haven't done anything wrong, so don't worry about it."

He followed her to the parlor. Tolliver stood, when they entered. Jonas said, "This is Mr. Tolliver. My daughter, Mary Catherine."

"Miss Parsons, it is a pleasure meeting you. Do you mind if I call you Mary?"

She shook her head, nervous about this stranger talking to her. "You knew Samuel Chandler, I believe?"

"Yes sir," she said softly.

"You know he passed away recently?"

"Yes sir. We went to the funeral," she said, still puzzled.

"Mr. Chandler left a will, with you as a beneficiary."

She looked at Jonas. "It means he left something for you."

"There were two beneficiaries. Mr. Weathers was left a sizable amount of cash. The rest of his estate comes to you."

"I don't know what that means," she said.

"I think what Mr. Tolliver is saying is the Circle C Ranch, its buildings, cattle and other assets now belong to you," Jonas said.

She didn't grasp the enormity of what she had just been told.

"Mr. Chandler thought quite highly of you," Tolliver said. "I have had the privilege of being Mr. Chandler's attorney for many years. He had no relatives, but when he had me draw it up, he said he thought of you as a granddaughter. He also spoke of the many kindnesses you showed him. In addition to the ranch and its assets there is a sizable bank account. Mary Catherine, you are a wealthy young lady.

"I will need for you to come to my office and I'll prepare the documents for probate. You may bring your attorney if you like. In fact, I would advise it."

"I don't have one," she replied.

"The attorney who did the work when we adopted you is our attorney," Jonas told her. "He represents you also."

"Good, good," Tolliver said. "Would next Friday be a satisfactory time?"

"It will," Jonas said. "I will notify our attorney. It will be before Judge Horner, I guess."

"Yes, Judge Horner handles probate too," Tolliver said. "It's been a real pleasure meeting you, Miss Parsons. Sam was a friend of mine, and I know the high regard he held for you."

"Thank you, Mr. Tolliver. I appreciate what you said. I really liked Mr. Sam, and his passing saddened me."

"That concludes our business, Mr. Parsons, a pleasure meeting you, sir, Miss Parsons."

CHAPTER TWENTY

Why

"I don't understand, Papa," Mary Catherine said. "Why did he do this? Why didn't he leave it to Mr. Weathers? He's worked for him for years."

"I don't have an answer, but he was touched by your kindness to him."

"I didn't do anything, we just talked."

"That was a kindness. There aren't very many young people who pay much attention to an older person not related to them. Where you came from and how you turned out is amazing. It makes you a special person."

"I'm just a girl who likes helping people."

"In my eyes, you're a very special person. Sam felt the same way."

"Aw Papa, that's sweet of you to say."

"I mean every word."

"I don't know anything about business, let alone ranching. What do I do?"

"I have a suggestion. Let's talk to Clint Weathers about running it for you. Pay him more, and turn it over to him. I believe he's already living in the ranch house with his wife. Unless you want to move, continue with things the way they are. I imagine he already has the hire and fire responsibilities. Sam did most of his buying, so let Clint handle that too. I don't know how Sam kept his records, but if you want to, you can use the same man who keeps our records to keep yours.

"You could also sell the entire operation. I personally don't believe in selling land. Another thing to consider, is you will probably have the money to do anything in the world you want, such as study to be a doctor or nurse."

"The only thing I want is to be your and Mama's daughter."

"I could almost cry over that, but I'm a cowboy, and cowboys don't cry."

The next Friday, Jonas and Emma accompanied Mary Catherine to Phineas Tolliver's office, where they were met by the Parsons' attorney, Philip Barnes.

"I've gone over the papers with Phineas," Barnes said, "and they are in order, as I expected. Sam's will was witnessed and straight forward. The transfer of the ranch and the bank accounts are ready for Judge Horner's signature. His clerk will let us know when he's ready to see us."

* * *

The First National Bank...

Attorney Barnes, accompanied them to the bank and presented the documents signed by Judge Horner, authorizing the transfer of any and all assets to Mary Catherine. She signed the papers required by the bank.

"Miss Parsons, the account is now in your name," Chester Good, the banker said. "I will bring the accounts so you can go through them."

She looked at Jonas. "I won't know what I'm looking at," she said.

"Mr. Good will go through them," Jonas said, and I can help."

"There are actually two accounts, one for ranch operations and the other was a personal account. The amounts in both are substantial.

She glanced at the figures at the bottom of the journal. "That's how much there is?"

"In that account, yes," said Chester.

"I didn't know there was that much money in the whole world," she said.

"Will you continue to do business with us, or will you be moving it."

"I suggest you keep them here," Jonas said. "Chester is an honest man and has handled our affairs for years."

"Lettie recommended him to me when I first came here," Emma said.

"Chester, who has access to the ranch account?" Jonas asked.

"Now? Just Mary Catherine. Sam handled both himself."

"I suggest you transfer some of this to the other account," Jonas said. "Then give Clint Weathers access to this one to meet the ranch payroll and other expenses. It's the way I do things for Thunder Canyon."

"Papa, I'm lost. Can't you just tell him what to do?"

"Honey, I could do that, however, I think it's important for you to stay involved, and know what you have."

"But I wouldn't know what I'm doing," she said. "Please?"

"What your father is trying to do is avoid any signs of impropriety," the banker said. "It's sound advice. The bank will act in your behalf for a small fee and I will scrutinize any activity. We are a national bank and our operations are controlled by the Federal Government even though Montana isn't a state."

"Good advice, Chester. Mary Catherine?"

"Yes sir. I will do that."

"Will you want any funds from the account today?" Chester asked.

"What would I do with money? I've never had any."

Emma laughed. "That's all changed now. "You are still our daughter and are our responsibility. What you have is independent of us."

"Our next order of business is to meet with Clint Weathers," Jonas said. "I don't know how he is going to take all of this."

"I hope he's not angry at me. I didn't ask for any of it."

"You don't worry about it. I will handle it," Jonas said, "but I want you to be there."

Circle C Ranch...

Clint and Maude Weathers greeted them from the porch when they arrived at the Circle C. "We've been wondering when we would see you," Clint said.

"Sad times," Jonas said.

"I was the one that found him," Maude said. "Other than saying he was tired, everything was normal when he went to bed. He had been going over the books after supper. He was normally up before sunrise, but he took most of his meals with the hands because he considered it a waste to have someone fix for one person. When he didn't show up this morning, I went looking for him."

"Do you know about his will?" Jonas asked.

"I witnessed it," Clint said.

"Mary Catherine is uncomfortable about it."

"You needn't be," Clint said.

"Mr. Weathers, he shouldn't have done this. I don't deserve it, and I didn't ask for it."

"We know that," Clint said. "From the time he met you in the hospital, he had a new light in his eyes. He told us about you talking to him long into the night, and he was determined to see you were taken care of."

"Papa takes care of me," she said.

"He told Maude and me he would have adopted you but was afraid of how it would look since he was alone in the house."

"I thought you and Maude were staying in the house," Jonas said.

"No sir, he built a house for us some years ago. He lived alone, though we ate with him once or twice a week. He preferred it that way. The house keeper does have a room behind the kitchen though.

"Missy, don't you fret none about what he did. He was very generous to us in his will. We're quite satisfied with everything."

"Thank you, Mr. Weathers. I was worried about it," Mary Catherine said.

"Clint, the decisions are Mary Catherine's, but I've made several suggestions to her. First, we hope you're not thinking of leaving."

"No sir. This is home."

"I suggested that all operations of the ranch be put in your hands, the hiring and firing as well as the ranch management. It will be more responsibility for you, and your pay will be increased to account for it.

"We thought you were living in the house here, and planned to continue to do so. I hope she doesn't decide to leave us and come here, but anyway that's her decision too. I have an accountant that manages the books for Thunder Canyon, and I suggested she do the same. I'm not talking about breeding records and such, just the contracts. What do you think?"

"It sounds good to me, Mr. Parsons."

"Jonas please. Mr. Parsons was Papa."

"Mr. Weathers, would you and Miss Maude be more comfortable in this house? It would be a shame to have it sit empty. I don't plan to live here, at least until Mama and Papa make me leave."

"That's mighty generous," Clint said. "We'd just rattle around in here though. It was a shame Sam and Cora never had children because it's why he built such a large house."

"Mr. Weathers, you've made me feel so much better. Thank you," Mary Catherine said.

"Thank you for being so kind to Sam. He was a good man."

"He was. He was the very first friend I ever had. Ever."

Planning

Have you done any thinking about things you might want to have or do, or places you might want to go?" Emma asked.

"I have everything I want," Mary Catherine said.

"In order to be a teacher in Ohio, I had to go to college. I had to finish high school in order to get into college. I know you learned to read and write in the orphanage. Did they have grades or anything?"

"No ma'am. The sisters taught us."

"What did you learn besides reading and writing?

"It wasn't a real school. I mean we had classes and history and learned about the Church, and its beliefs. Sister Louisa and the Mother Superior were very strict with us about learning, and we had class every day except Saturday and Sunday.

"So did you graduate from high school?"

"I don't have any way of proving it, but I believe I have a good education."

"Would you be willing to take a test to see if you have the same level as they require to graduate?" Emma asked.

"Why would I do that?"

"If you decided you wanted to go to college, then you'd have proof."

"What's college like?"

"I went to the Ohio Normal School which is a college to train teachers, which is the only thing I ever wanted to be. Well, except to be a mother."

"If you think I should, then I will."

"I think it would be a good idea, and it certainly won't hurt anything," Emma said. "The next time we go into town, we can look into it. I don't know what they would ask, because I taught first grade."

Are there any colleges in Helena?"

"I don't think there is one in the entire territory. I would be surprised if there is one in Wyoming either. Nebraska has one and the University of Denver is excellent."

"Aren't they a long way from here?"

"Denver is all day on a train. I don't know long it would take to get to Nebraska."

"We came through it on the mercy train, but I have no idea about the time. How long is college?"

"It depends on the program. I went four years, but there are also two year programs."

"That's a long time," Mary Catherine said.

"You only go nine months out of the year. They usually start in September and go through June."

"That's still a long time."

"It is, but for me, it was worth it. I had a dream, and it was the path to my dream."

"I'm living my dream," Mary Catherine said.

"You have a long life ahead of you. A life without dreams would be empty."

"You aren't teaching now, so you don't have your dream."

"That's where you're wrong. Being a mother was another dream. When Lettie is old enough to go to school, I plan to teach again, if not before then. I want to see all of my children go to college. They may not all want to, but I'd like to see it."

"Me too?"

"You're my daughter, aren't you?"

"Yes ma'am."

Two days later, Mary Catherine asked Emma to find out what she had to do."

* * *

Emma helped Mary Catherine with a letter to the Registrar of the University of Nebraska asking for an application.

It took a month, but she finally received an application. In another month she received an acceptance letter.

"We'll go to Lincoln and get you enrolled and settled in," Jonas said.

"If they don't have on-campus housing, we'll have to find an apartment or a boarding house." Emma said. "Since you have never lived alone or on your own, I'll worry about you. It might be easier for you if you had a roommate." "You're accustomed to being around people and you get along well. You have a kind heart, and trust everyone, but unfortunately not all people are good, and some of them are just plain bad. A young woman is prey to them. I ran into some of that when Papa passed."

The trip was long. It was after dark when they arrived. A hotel put them up for the night.

At the office of the registrar, Mary Catherine was enrolled. She chose farm and ranching as her course of study. "Do you have on campus housing?" Jonas asked.

"We don't for female students. We do keep a list of available housing that we have found to be satisfactory. Would you like to make a copy of the list?"

"I would, thank you," Jonas replied.

"Do you also have a list of anyone looking for a roommate?" Emma asked.

"As a matter of fact, we do," the man said. "We cannot vouch for them, however. We don't have a way to contact them either, so it doesn't do much good."

They looked at five places before one met Emma and Jonas's approval. "Let's talk about it over lunch," Emma suggested.

"The last place we saw was clean," Emma said, "and I liked the landlady. She was pleasant and seems to be a responsible person. Three of the places we saw didn't serve meals, and that bothers me because you would need to shop and cook for yourself. I'm afraid that would lead to you skipping meals, which is not a healthy situation. The other place I just did not like. What do you think?" she asked Mary Catherine.

"I liked Mrs. Healy," Mary Catherine agreed. "I'm afraid you're right about the cooking. I would probably find it was too much trouble to cook or to go to a restaurant.

"I wonder if any of the people there are students?"

"From my standpoint, I think the room needs a new bed, but that isn't a problem, we can get one," Jonas said. "It also needs a desk and chair."

"Do you think it will do?" Emma asked her daughter.

"Yes ma'am. It will be fine."

"We'll go back and see Mrs. Healy in the morning," Jonas said.

Next morning...

"You came back!" Mrs. Healy said.

"Mary Catherine decided she liked the idea of not having to cook," Emma said.

"My cooking isn't fancy, but it is wholesome."

"Mrs. Healy, are there any other students here?" Mary asked.

"Actually, there are," she said. "The house is ladies only, and three of the five boarders are students. Two of them share a room. The other girl is looking for a roommate. Would you be interested? I would have to put you in the larger room."

"Can I meet her?"

"I believe she's in the front parlor now. I'll introduce you," Mrs. Healy offered.

Julia Bedford was five feet, four inches. She had brown hair and an infectious grin, and was from Omaha. "Julia, This is Mary Catherine. She's going to be staying with us," Mrs. Healy said. "She might be looking for a roommate."

"Why don't you girls get acquainted while we have a cup of coffee?" Mrs. Healy said. She led Emma and Jonas to the kitchen. "Julia is a nice girl. She was here last year, and was disappointed when her roommate didn't come back for this year. She's a quiet girl and doesn't talk very much."

"Mary Catherine is pretty much the same way," Emma said.

In the parlor...

"Did you go to school somewhere else last year?" Julia asked.

"No. I just recently decided to go to college. Mama was a teacher and convinced me it was a good thing to do."

"I'm going to be a teacher," Julia said. "What are you going to do?"

"Mama taught first grade, but stopped when her babies were born. She's planning to start again when the Joshua starts school. I didn't want to be a teacher or a nurse. I'm studying farm and ranch management," Mary Catherine said.

"You'll probably be the only girl in the class. The girls I know are all going to be teachers or nurses."

"I thought about nursing, but after I was adopted, I changed my mind."

"My aunt and uncle adopted a boy from the orphan train. We couldn't believe it when Aunt Ethel told us."

"I was on the orphan train," Mary Catherine said.

"What happened to your parents?"

Mary Catherine didn't answer. "It was nice meeting you," she told Julia, and went to find her parents.

Can We Forget It?

Later...

"What did you think?" Emma asked.

"I believe I prefer to not have a roommate," Mary Catherine said. "Maybe one of the other places would be better for me."

"May I ask why you feel that way?"

"Some of the questions she asked, and things she said bothered me."

"What was said?" Emma asked.

"She's going to be a teacher and asked what I was going to do. When I told her, she said all of the girls here were either going to be nurses or teachers, and I would be the only girl in the classes. I told her I had thought about nursing but after I was adopted, I changed my mind.

"She said her aunt and uncle had adopted a boy from the orphan train. She said they couldn't believe it when her aunt told them they were adopting. The way she said it was like it was something to be ashamed of."

"I told her I was on the train. I didn't say it, but it was probably the same train. Then she asked what happened to my parents. I didn't answer."

"She was probably curious and didn't even think about what she said. It might be better if you didn't tell people about your circumstances."

"Why not? I'm not ashamed of it."

"I'm sorry, honey. I should not have put it that way. It was thoughtless of me."

"Maybe I should just forget about this college thing, and go back home."

Jonas had been quiet during the conversation. "If you want to go back home, then we'll go back home, but don't let a thoughtless question be the reason.

"I agree with what your mother said, but I'm going to say it a little differently. The frontier is a harsh place, and a lot of the children here have lost at least one of their parents, and a lot of parents have lost more than one of their children. I've heard it said that one in ten people on the Oregon Trail died, so they are not surprised by someone missing a parent. Your circumstances were quite a bit different from those they know about, so it naturally arouses their curiosity, and curious people ask questions. The thing to do, is don't arouse their curiosity.

"The fact that you own a ranch is unusual, and you would have suitors lining the road to court you if it became common knowledge. It would probably be a good idea not to bring that up either. You would probably have all sorts of people coming out of the woodwork trying to help you spend your money. It isn't fair, but life isn't fair. It's the way it is, and we have to play the cards dealt to us."

"You are a smart man, Papa."

"Why do you think I married him?" Emma asked.

"He's handsome?" Mary Catherine replied with a smile.

"There is that," Emma agreed.

"I do like this better than the other places, but I would like a room to myself."

"Then that's what you should do," Jonas said. I will make the arrangements with Mrs. Healy. Would you rather have the larger room, or the one we saw first?"

"The small one is fine. I don't have much."

"Mrs. Healy, is there a difference in the large room and the smaller one, other than size?" Jonas asked.

"The large room has a bathtub, where the smaller one would share the tub with the others. Both have a sink."

"We'll take the large one then. Do you object to us getting a new bed and a desk? At our expense of course."

"So she is going to room with Julia?" Mrs. Healy asked.

"Mary Catherine decided not to have a roommate. She would like more privacy."

"That's too bad."

"Is it going to be a problem for you? We don't want to cause you any trouble."

"It is not a problem for me. Julia is going to be disappointed because it would have reduced her cost. The large room rents for more."

"We expected that. We will pay for the entire school term in advance so she doesn't have to worry about it."

"I'll get the rent agreement and the house rules."

"What are your house rules?"

"I don't allow men in the house, and no parties. If that is violated, they will not be allowed to remain. The rooms must be kept clean. Clean bedding every week. Meal times are set and observed. Nothing unusual."

"As a father, that makes me happy," Jonas said.

"The mister and I weren't blessed with children, and I try to treat the girls here as my own. When will she be moving in?"

"Tomorrow. We are going to buy a new bed and a desk. My wife and I will return home the day after that.

"Mrs. Healy, I feel comfortable trusting my daughter to your care," Emma said. "Thank you."

After they left, Mary Catherine said, "Papa, this should come from the money in Mr. Sam's account."

"It is your account, and my children do not pay for their education. It is my responsibility. We will go to the bank this afternoon and set up an account for you. It will be enough to cover your expenses and will be replenished."

"Papa, I'm grateful, but it isn't necessary for you to do this."

"When you became my daughter, I assumed the responsibility for your care and wellbeing. This is part of it. It will be the same for your brothers and sisters when it's their time."

"I don't know why God has smiled on me so much," she said.

"You are His child too, and are deserving of no less."

The new bed and desk were delivered, and it was time for Emma and Jonas to return home. Mary

Catherine accompanied them to the train station. The tearful departure marked the first time she had been separated from her family since they met.

"You're strong and have good instincts," Emma said. "You'll be fine."

"Show them how it's done in Montana," Jonas said. "If you have any problems, anything at all, send a telegram, and I'll be on the next train. I spoke with Mrs. Healy and she's promised to keep an eye out for you. I'm proud of you for taking this on. We love you and you're an important member of our family."

"I love you and Mama too. I'm proud to be a Parsons."

She stood on the platform until the train was out of sight. *It was hard seeing them leave. I don't have anyone to lean on. I've been alone before. I'll make it.* She trudged back to her room.

Where's Mary Catherine?

"I'm going to ask Mary Catherine if I can call on her," Trace Jennings told his mother.

"Good for you," she said. "It's about time you did something. When did you decide this?"

"I've been thinking about it for a long time, but could never find the words. I'm just going to come out and ask her."

"As pretty as she is, I wouldn't be surprised if she isn't already courting."

"Me either, but I don't know anyone close around here she would be courting."

"They do have the house in town, so maybe someone in town is courting her. Her family is comfortable, so that would attract men like flies to honey."

"She's adopted. She wouldn't stand to get what their real kids get."

"I swan, sometimes I wonder if you're really my child. I garntee if you ask Jonas, he'll tell you she's the same as the others to him and Emma."

Church...

"Howdy, Mrs. Parsons," Trace said. "Did Mary Catherine come with you this morning?"

"Mary Catherine is in college. She won't be coming home until the Christmas break."

"College? Where?"

"She is at the University of Nebraska," Emma said.

"Why did she go that far away?"

"There are no colleges in Montana or Wyoming. We preferred Nebraska over Denver."

"I don't think I know of anyone that went to college."

"I did," Emma replied.

"How long is college?"

"She's studying farm and ranch management. There's a two year program and a four year program. She's starting out in the two year program, but may switch."

"Do you write to her?" he asked.

"Yes, regularly."

"Would you tell her I asked about her?"

"Why don't you write? She would love to hear from you. I can give you her address."

"Shucks, I couldn't talk to her when she was standing in front of me. I wouldn't have no idea what to say in a letter."

"It should be easier in a letter," Emma said. "You just say what you've been doing, who you saw, and what the weather is like. You're getting ready for your roundup, so you could write about that. It's just like talking except you're putting it on paper. I'll write her address down for you."

Back home...

"Mary Catherine is in Nebraska going to college," Trace said. "She won't be home until Christmas, and then she goes back. Miss Emma said she's studying farming and ranching, and she will be gone at least two years."

"That's too bad. What are you going to do?"

"I've been thinking about putting an ad in the paper."

"Lettie Owens told me there are a few around. I recollect hearing about it, but I don't any of the names."

"I might as well give it a try."

"What about the address Emma gave you? Are you going to write her?"

"I don't know. I've never written a letter before. I am going to ask Silas if he knows how I can get one of those marriage newspapers. Since the post office is in his store, he probably knows."

Mrs. Healy's Boarding House...

When Mary Catherine answered the tap on her door, it was Julia Bedford. "Come in, I just finished unpacking and putting things away."

"I thought you were looking for a roommate," Julia said. "What happened?"

"Mama had suggested it might be easier since I'm away from home for the first time. I have my own room at the ranch, and it's bigger than this one, and I decided with two people it might get crowded."

"I couldn't afford this one by myself," Julia said. "A roommate would have made it possible. What happened to the other bed? There were two in here."

"When I decided not to have a roommate, Mrs. Healy took them out, and Papa got a new one for me. I wanted to have a desk, so I have more room this way."

"Do you get everything you want?" Julia asked.

"No, I don't. I have two brothers and two sisters, and all of us except the baby have chores.

"Julia, I seem to have offended you in some way. I am sorry for whatever it was. I was hoping we could be friends. I've never had a friend close to my age, and I wanted to be your friend."

"It's not you. I was disappointed when I saw you moving in alone. I would like to be friends. Sometimes I can be a little abrupt without even knowing it. I shouldn't have been asking you those questions."

"It's okay," Mary Catherine said. "I'm not embarrassed I was an orphan. Mama told me right after I came to live with them, I should remember they had a choice and chose me to be their daughter. All of us are treated the same too. I'm very lucky, and I have the kindest, nicest parents in the world."

"I don't know," Julia said. "Mine are pretty special."

"Do you have brothers and sisters?"

"No, I have always wished I had a sister. Sometimes there are things you just don't want to talk about with your mother."

"I've only had mine for a little over two years and have never had anything I felt uncomfortable talking about."

"Why do you want to study farm management? I live on a farm and don't want any part of it."

"I worked in Saint John's Hospital when I first got to Montana, and I didn't like to see the pain and suffering, so that ruled nursing out. I was in Catholic Schools, and the only teachers they had were nuns."

"How was it?" Julia asked.

"Strict," Mary Catherine said. "If you did something they didn't like, you'd get rapped across your knuckles with a ruler. It hurt too."

Lazy J Ranch...

After four tries that resulted in wadded up paper, Trace had an ad he thought was close enough to the ones in the paper.

Twenty three year old male, 5 feet, 9 inches, dark hair and weight of 160 pounds. Able to read and write, desires correspondence with a female of same approximate age with proportional weight. Must be able to read and write.

He signed it, and stuffed it into an envelope to be mailed on his next trip into town. *I'm not going to tell mama about this. I don't want her to tell me how to do it. This is my doing.*

He handed the letter to Silas. "I'd just as soon Mama didn't know about this," he said.

"It's the U.S. Mail and is private. I don't discuss it with anyone," Silas said.

"Good. How long will it take?"

"Well, it will go out on the next train. The others I've seen take a couple of months before anything comes back."

"Thank you," Trace said. "I'll get the supplies loaded into the wagon."

Welcome Home

It was cold when the train approached Helena. A snowfall the night before coated the ground, lending a pristine look to the surrounding area. The cattle in the pastures huddled together for communal warmth.

Sparks shot in a steady shower from under the wheels, caused by the metal to metal contact between the driving wheels of the locomotive and the cold steel of the tracks. Clouds of steam rolled from under the boiler, and smoke and cinders spewed from the stack on top of the locomotive. With a long sigh, the train came to a stop.

Mary Catherine donned her heavy coat, and grabbed the valise she had brought with her. Her trunk had been checked through at Lincoln. Mattie ran to her as she stepped onto the wooden platform. Mary Catherine set her valise down and hugged her sister. "I missed you, Mattie. I thought about you every day. You've gotten prettier and you've grown since I left."

Mattie hugged her fiercely. "I missed you too. Do you have to go back?"

"Not until after Christmas. I have four weeks at home before I have to go back."

The rest of the family gathered around. Mary Catherine hugged each of her siblings, even Little Jonas, who was not normally given to displays of affection.

Her mother was holding Joshua, so she hugged both of them. "It's so good to see all of you. I missed you all so much, I've been marking the days off on my calendar.

"Papa." She went into his open arms. "It feels so good to hug you again."

She was reluctant to break the contact until he asked, "Did you check any baggage?"

"Just my small trunk."

"I'll get it and put it in the wagon," he said.

Bundled with buffalo robes they left Helena for the hour's drive to the Thunder Canyon Ranch.

Mattie chattered away to no one in particular, while Mary Catherine, with Lettie in her lap and Emma, holding Joshua talked. No one noticed the cold.

"Lord have mercy, jes look at you," Pearlie May said. "You is a sight for these sore old eyes. Stand back and let me look at you."

She hugged Mary Catherine to her ample bosom. "It's good to have you home."

"It's good to be home, Miss Pearlie May."

"I'm gonna fix you a special dinner tonight."

"That sounds good," Mary Catherine said. "Mrs. Healy is a good cook, but no one cooks like you."

"I wish you would listen to this girl. She trying to get more. I might have to fry up another chicken jes for her."

Later...

"We didn't decorate the tree yet because I remembered how much pleasure you got from it last year," Emma said.

"We got one," Little Jonas said. "Me and Papa cut it down."

"Papa and I," Emma corrected.

"Yeah, Papa and I." he said. "We cut it down. It's in the barn. Papa made the thing to make it stand up."

"Mama said we can put the things on it after supper," Mattie said. "You have to do the high things because I can't reach them."

"We make a good team don't we," Mary said.

"Uh huh."

"I almost forgot. I brought something for you, all of the way from Nebraska. I'll go get them."

She returned with a small doll with a bisque head for Mattie and one for Lettie. "Remember when you gave me Miss Betsy?" she asked Mattie.

Mattie nodded. "She slept in my bed every night while I was gone, so I decided to pay you back. This is for you, and the other one is for Lettie."

"What about me?" Jonas asked.

"I didn't think you would want a doll, so I brought this for you. It's called a yo-yo. I practiced with it so I could show you how it works." After she demonstrated it, she handed it to him."

"Thanks, Mary Catherine. Do I have to wait until Christmas?"

"No," she said. "That's for now. There's something else for Christmas. Mama, you and Papa are going to have to wait until Christmas for yours."

"That was sweet of you to remember them," Emma said.

"I thought about all of you every day," Mary Catherine said.

"Before I forget, Trace Jennings asked about you. I gave him your address. Did he ever write?"

"No ma'am."

"That's too bad. I thought he might."

"The only mail I got was from you. I just about wore them out, I read them so many times."

"It will be nice when we get the telephone here. We plan to have a line run out here as soon as it's available. Then we will be able to talk to you."

"There's no telephone in the house. Mrs. Healy said she doesn't need one."

"If you're still in school when we get one here, then we'll have one installed in your room, if Mrs. Healy allows it," Jonas said.

"Have you made any friends?" Emma asked.

"Julia and I are good friends now. She's going to be a teacher by the way. She still doesn't understand why I don't want to do that or be a nurse. I haven't told her anything about the Circle C."

"That's a good idea," Jonas said. "I've been talking to Clint regularly. He's doing a good job for you. You had a good roundup and I think we both had a good breeding season."

Her face colored. "At first I was kind of embarrassed when the professor talked about that. I thought everyone was watching how I would react when it was brought up. Then I realized it was something they had been seeing all of their lives. After that, it didn't bother me.

"We started reading about crossbreeding right before the end of the term. It is on the schedule for next term."

"What are they crossbreeding?" Jonas asked.

"The Longhorn and the Hereford," she said.

"What's wrong with the Longhorn?"

The professor said the Longhorn meat is tough and stringy. He said for the same cost, the Hereford produces a lot more meat."

"That's interesting," Jonas said. "When you get back, if you can find more information, I would be interested in reading about it."

"Can we find something more interesting than cattle breeding to talk about?" Emma asked.

"Hey, you've got two ranchers here, what do you expect us to talk about?" Jonas asked.

CHAPTER TWENTY-FIVE

Christmas

Sunday...

The weather was clear but cold. The road to town was in good shape, so Jonas decided they would go into town, stay in their house over the weekend, then go to church and visit their friends.

Mary Catherine visited Sister Anne at the hospital. "I'm very pleased you have the opportunity to continue your education," Sister Anne said. "The Heavenly Father is smiling upon you."

"He truly is, Sister. I have to go, Mama is expecting me back. We are going shopping this afternoon. It is good to see you again."

Her next stop was the parsonage. She found Lettie and Jack busy getting the sanctuary ready for the next day's services.

"Can I help?" Mary Catherine asked, entering the sanctuary. Lettie had a scarf tied around her beautiful hair, and was wearing an apron. She had a feather duster in her hand.

"Mary Catherine, I thought you might be coming home this weekend. It is so good to see you. I have included you in my nightly prayers, and here you are." They hugged.

"We're staying in town this weekend and will be at church tomorrow, so I came to help you clean a seat for us."

"All help is greatly appreciated and welcome," Lettie said. "How is school?"

"It was hard to get used to in the beginning, but I've learned how to study and it is going well now. I have a nice room in a boarding house for women, and I've made a few friends. Of course I miss my family, and it was good to see them again. I have almost four weeks at home before I have to return."

"Have you met any young men?"

"I'm the only girl in the class," Mary said, "so I know their names, but there is no one special for me."

"Someday someone special will come along, and you'll know it when he does."

"I hope he waits until I finish school," Mary said.

Lettie laughed. "Just remember, the ways of God are many. We don't always get what we want. Sometimes we get what is best for us."

"I told Julia about you, and how wonderful you've been for me."

"Is she your roommate?"

"No ma'am. Her room is down the hall from me. I room alone."

"It's good you've found a friend. Thank you for your help. Would you like some refreshment?"

"No ma'am. Momma and I are going shopping this afternoon, but I'll see you in the morning. It's been nice seeing you again."

"Good to see you too," Lettie said.

The next morning…

The Sunday morning visiting usually took place outside, but with the chill in the air, they were in the narthex. "When did you come home," the dark haired young man asked.

"Trace! I got back the day before yesterday. How are you?"

"I'm fine, just dreading the coming winter though. Did you mother tell you I had asked about you?"

"She wrote me about it. That was nice of you."

"I was going to write a letter, but I didn't know what to say, or whether you would like it or not."

"It would have been nice to hear from you," she said. "The only mail I get is from Mama."

"Are you all finished with school?"

"No," she laughed. "I'm half-way through the first year, so I have another year and a half to go, unless I decide to go through the four year program, then it would be three and a half."

"That's a long time."

"It is," she replied, "and I miss my family, so I'm probably going to get the two year degree."

"What are you learning?"

"All about the business end of ranching and farming. Contracts and things like that. Do you do that for your ranch?"

"No, Mama handles all of that," he said.

"I want to be able to help Papa with that part of it."

Can't he show you how?"

"He could, but there are so many things happening so fast, we want to be able to keep up with it."

The sounds of the piano signaled it was time for them to take their seats. "Uh... uh... Mary Catherine, would it be all right if I sit with you this morning?"

"Yes, I would like that. You may have to fight Mattie though. She likes to sit beside me. She can sit on the other side, and Lettie can sit next to Mama."

Emma nodded to Trace and slid closer to her husband to make room.

"Maybe I'll see you again while you're home," Trace said.

"Probably," she said. "Thanks for sitting with us. I enjoyed talking to you. It's always nice to have company."

"Maybe I could come visit some day when the weather is good."

"That would be nice."

He retrieved his heavy coat and began looking for his mother."

"I saw you sitting with Mary Catherine," she said. "What was that all about?"

"Nothing, I asked if I could sit with her and she said she would like that, so I did."

"What about that mail order woman you wrote?"

"I don't even know her name or where she lives. Besides, it will probably be another month before I get another letter."

"Did you tell Mary Catherine about her?"

"Not really," he said.

"Either you did or you didn't. Son, you need to concentrate on one thing at a time."

"Mary Catherine will be going back to Nebraska in three weeks. I was just talking to her. Don't make such a big fuss about it."

"You watch your mouth, young man. I'm still your mama."

"Yes ma'am."

Another letter…

"I have a letter for you," Silas Farmer told Trace two days after Christmas.

Dear Number 1643

I have been rereading your letters and have given it a lot of thought. I think we should meet and get acquainted.

My name is Christine Pogue, and I am from Canton, Ohio. I am hoping you will tell me your name and where you live. I have enjoyed your letters very much and you sound like the kind of person I would like to know. Please write me directly. It takes so long to go through the newspaper.

Sincerely,

Christine Pogue

He read the letter three times, and decided to show it to his mother. "Well, this is certainly something to think about. How many letters have you had?"

"This is the third one."

"To meet, you would pay her way to Helena, is that right?"

"Yes ma'am, and for her meals on the way. If we like one another, we would get married. If we don't, I would have to pay for her return trip."

"What's to keep her from just taking the money and not coming?" Sadie asked.

"Nothing, I guess. She doesn't sound like that kind of person. She's had a hard time of it. She's been a housekeeper to help her mother. Her father didn't come back from the war, just like Papa."

"You don't know all of that is true," Sadie said.

"True enough, but she doesn't know what I wrote was true either," he said.

"If that's what it takes for you to find a wife, then go ahead, just use a little bit of caution," she advised.

He answered the letter after checking with the railroad on travel times and costs.

Dear Christine,

My name is Trace Jennings. My father was killed in the war, and my mother and I own a nice cattle ranch outside Helena, Montana.

I have checked with the railroad and it would take two and one-half days to get from Canton to Helena. I will provide transportation and expenses from Canton to Helena and return fare if things don't work out. If that is agreeable, please let me know and I will send the funds by Western Union. You would have them the day after I send it. You can let me know the day of your arrival and I will meet the train.

"I'm excited by the idea of meeting you and look forward to your visit.

Sincerely,

Trace Jennings

Lazy J Ranch

Helena, Montana

"Silas, will you make sure this gets in the next mail?" Trace asked.

"I will put it in the bag myself," Silas promised.

CHAPTER TWENTY-SIX

Embarrassed

It was the arrival day.

Wearing his best Sunday-go-to-meeting clothes, Trace was at the depot forty-five minutes before the train was due. The telegrapher told him it was on time, so he settled in to wait.

He brushed imaginary dust from his Stetson hat and checked the mirror. He heard the whistle off in the distance and went back to the platform. The train stopped, brakes squealing. The engine huffed and released pressure from the boiler, steam shot from beneath as it waited for the engineer's hand to move the throttle and set it in motion again.

Trace watched the passengers step onto the platform. There were only three women among them, and they were with men who appeared to be their husbands. He went to the conductor.

"Excuse me sir," he said. "I'm looking for a young woman who would be traveling from Ohio alone. Did I miss her?"

"There were no women traveling alone on this train."

"You must be mistaken. She sent word she would be on this train, today," Trace said.

"I've been on this train since Saint Louis, and there have been no unaccompanied young ladies. The ladies you just saw boarded in Kansas City."

Disheartened, he went home. "She wasn't on the train," he told his mother. "She must have missed it, I don't think I got the dates mixed up."

Two weeks passed before he received another letter.

Dear Trace,

I am sorry I was unable to come. My mother came down with influenza, and there was no one to take care of her. She didn't get any better and last Friday, she joined Papa in heaven.

I had no money to pay the undertaker so I had to use what you sent for the ticket. I am so sorry, but don't you worry, I will use my butter and egg money to repay you so you won't be out anything. You will get every penny, I promise.

"I fear I will be unable to come meet you because there is no one to take care of my brother. Caleb is a

real hard worker and would probably be a lot of help around your ranch if he came there. He isn't old enough to get a real paying job.

I will understand if you want to change your mind, but I couldn't help it. It was Mama and me alone in the world after Papa died in the war.

Sincerely,

Christine Pogue

Not wanting to hear the 'I told you so', Trace did not show his mother the latest letter. She was asking for fare for her brother, as well as another fare for himself. Sleep did not come easy that night. He finally arrived at a decision.

I'm going to send her the money. Having to bury her mother is a good reason for not coming the first time. A person has to take care of family. If he was my only kin, I would want my brother to come too. I couldn't just go off and leave him. She's really a caring person, I hope she likes the Lazy J... and me.

He wired the money the next day, along with a message asking her to send him the arrival date by return wire. He heard nothing in return.

"Did you ever hear any more from that girl?" Sadie asked.

"Which girl?" he asked innocently.

"The one you sent the money to; who do you think I'm talking about?"

"I thought you might be talking about Mary Catherine," he said.

"You haven't written her, why would she be writing you?"

"She hasn't written to me, so why would I be writing her?"

"You're getting smart mouth again," she said.

"Mama, you know I love you as much as you love me, but it's getting downright tiresome with you always talking about me getting a wife. I tried, and she took the money and didn't come. What am I supposed to do, keep sending money to strangers?"

* * *

"Miss Emma, will Mary Catherine be home for Easter?" Trace asked.

"I'm afraid not, I wish she could, but there isn't enough time to make the trip."

"When will school be out?" he asked.

"June, but she's thinking about taking some classes during the summer to save time. If she does that, she will come home for a couple of weeks, and go back until the end of July."

"I was hoping to see her during Easter," he said.

"Have you told her that?"

"No ma'am."

"How is she supposed to know? I'm going to give you some motherly advice, even though I'm not your mother. Girls are funny. If you don't tell them something, then they don't know. Girls like for boys to compliment them on their appearance, their hair or their dress, their smile. One difference between girls and boys is that girls are all about feelings, while boys are about doing. They like to talk about things while boys like to do things.

"Let me give you an example. What do you think about when you see a horse running like the wind across a pasture?"

"I'd like to be riding him."

"I would think about how graceful he is and what a magnificent creature he is. Do you see the difference?"

"I think so."

"Every young man who wants a happy marriage needs to learn that. If you want to be happy, you don't think of a wife as a maid or a cook. Nor is she a laundress. She should be your partner. If you want to be happy, then she has to be happy first."

That evening…

His mother had gone to bed, and he had already banked the fire in the fireplace. Instead of going up the stairs, Trace went to the room they used for an office and sat at the desk. He took several sheets of paper and a pencil from the drawer. He chewed on the end of the pencil for a minute and began to write.

Letters

It was after midnight before he finally put the words on paper he wanted to say.

Dear Mary Catherine,

I hope this finds you well and in good spirits, and enjoying your school. Life on the Lazy J has pretty much the same thing happening every day. There was so much snow, the cattle couldn't get to the grass, so we had to haul hay out to the pastures. We had to break through the ice so they would have water. We will probably have to do it again in a couple of days. I'm hoping for an early thaw.

I spoke to your mother after church the other day. I was disappointed when she told me you would not be coming for Easter. I was hoping to see you. She told me you were also thinking about taking classes during the summer.

I would be pleased if you could find the time to write me. I would like to know about the things you are learning.

I don't know anything about college and have never known anyone that went.

I am hoping you decide to write.

Sincerely,

Trace Jennings

He read through what he had written. *It sounds like something a school boy would write. She will probably get a big laugh out of it, being around all of those college boys.*

He started to crumple it up and throw it in with his previous efforts. *I'm not going to do it. She probably won't answer it, but I'm going to mail it anyway. Maybe at least she will get a good laugh out of it.*

He couldn't mail it until he went to the mercantile for supplies the following Saturday. He handed it to Silas, along with the two pennies for postage. He waited for Silas to comment, but all he said was, "It will go out in the next mail."

Relieved, Trace handed him the list of supplies he needed. "I'm going to get a haircut," he told the store owner. "Newt will be here to help me load up."

"How are you fixed for hay?" Silas asked. I have a couple of names that have some if you need it."

"We're good, I think. Newt made sure we had plenty laid by. He checks the wooly worms to decide how much we might need."

"Some people swear by them," Silas said. "I put more store in the Farmer's Almanac."

Mrs. Healy's Boarding House...

"I don't believe it," Mary Catherine said after looking at the letter Mrs. Healy handed her. "He actually wrote."

"Is it from your beau?"

"No ma'am, he's a neighbor back home. We go to the same church, but I don't know him very well. Neither of us talk much. Mama told me she gave him my address, but that was before Christmas. It's the first letter I've ever had that didn't come from my family."

This is interesting. I am going to answer it. He was disappointed I won't be coming home for Easter. This is sweet. No one has ever said anything like this to me before.

Mary Catherine always went over the subjects covered during the day, as well as what was planned for the next day. She didn't have farm or ranch experience, and felt it a necessary thing in order to keep with those born on ranches and farms. When she closed the books, she opened the box of scented stationery her mother had given her for Christmas and took out two sheets.

Dear Trace,

I received your most welcome letter yesterday. It was a pleasant surprise to hear from you.

Mama told me about the snowfall and the cattle. I guess that is one of the hard parts about living on a ranch. Papa told me about how dumb cattle are. He said they would die of thirst before they would think to break the ice.

School is going very well, thank you for asking. We recently had a session on crossbreeding between Herefords and Longhorns. I believe Papa is going to look into it for the Thunder Canyon herd.

It is disappointing for me to miss Easter with the family, but the train trip is about sixteen hours each way and I have class on the Friday before and the Monday after Easter Sunday.

I have decided to attend summer school. By doing so, I can cut one full year off the four year program, and allow me to finish in three years. I do miss my family while I'm away, but what I'm learning will allow me to help Papa more, and to repay them in some small manner for all they have done for me.

Thank you again for writing. I enjoyed the letter and the news. Please write again.

Sincerely,

Mary Catherine

* * *

"Do I have any mail?" Trace asked Silas.

"I believe there might be something here for you," Silas replied. "Yessir, here is one. I recognize the envelope. Emma Parsons had me order the box of stationery for Mary Catherine last Christmas."

"It does look fancier than the ones I use," Trace said.

"Smells good too," Silas said, and handed the envelope to him.

Trace tucked the envelope inside of his shirt. "I think I'll save it until I get back home,"

Back at the ranch, he told his mother, "I have a letter from Mary Catherine Parsons."

"You do? I didn't know you had written her."

"I did, a couple of weeks ago."

"What did she have to say?"

"I don't know. I haven't read it yet," he said.

"I'm glad you wrote her. She's a sweet girl. Emma is very proud of her. She's still in college?"

"Yes ma'am. Going to be there two more years."

"Land sakes, she's going to be an old maid by the time she gets out. Twenty-three or twenty-four, not married and no beau. There must be plenty of boys in that college though. Emma told me she was the only girl, so she probably has her pick of them. I wouldn't be surprised to see her come back home with a husband."

Trace bit his tongue to keep from responding to what his mother was hinting. "I'm going to stretch out and read this before supper," he said.

The next day…

"Newt, have you ever seen any Herefords?" Trace asked his foreman.

"Yeah, I seen some when we drove the herd to Denver."

"What did you think about them?"

"They are shorter and wider than the Longhorns, so I guess they produce more meat. One thing for danged sure is they ain't as ornery as a Longhorn. Why are you asking about them?"

"I was thinking about mixing some in with our herd and see how it worked out."

"It might work," Newt said. "Wade Gentry told me they are going to put twenty Hereford bulls in with theirs."

"Jonas is a smart man. Maybe we should try it too. Be on the lookout for a place to get some."

Stranger at the Gate

The wagon approached the ranch house at the Lazy J. "Hello the house," the driver called out.

"I'll just go knock on the door," the passenger said.

"Ma'am out here, you don't get off your horse or out of the wagon until you're invited. It can get you shot."

"Surely you are joking."

"No ma'am, I ain't." He raised his voice, "Hello the house."

A man came around the corner of the house. "Mose, what are you doing way out here?"

"I brung you a visitor," the stable owner said.

"Are you Trace Jennings?" the lady asked.

"No ma'am. I'm Newt Hawkins. I'm the foreman. You want to see Trace?"

"Yes please."

"He's at the corral. I'll get him."

She started to get down from the wagon. The driver placed a restraining hand on her arm. "Ma'am, you ain't been invited."

"Well, I never," she exclaimed. "What kind of place is this?"

"It's Montana," was all he said. "Here comes Trace now."

"You know him?"

"Ever since he was a snot nose kid," Mose said.

"Howdy, Mose," the lanky cowboy said. "Newt said you brought a visitor."

"Visitors," Mose said. "They's two of them."

"I'm Christine Pogue. I thought you were going to meet us."

"Ma'am, I was at the depot the day you said, and you were not on the train, and I never heard from you again," he said defensively.

"I sent you a telegram telling you I was going to be delayed and giving you today's date."

"I didn't receive a telegram."

"Are you doubting my word?" she asked.

"No ma'am, I'm just telling you I didn't get a telegram," he said doggedly.

"Well, I sent one."

"Mose, thank you for bringing them out. Here's something for your trouble," Trace said, digging in his pocket for a coin.

"No trouble at all. You want me to take the trunk inside?"

"Just help me get it to the porch and I'll take it in," Trace said. He extended a helping hand to Christine. The boy with her looked like he might be six or seven years old. He hopped from the wagon.

"Are you a cowboy?" he asked.

"I reckon I am, Trace said. "What's your name?"

"Caleb Pogue."

Trace shook hands solemnly. "Pleased to meet you, Caleb. Y'all come on inside."

He led them into the parlor. "I'll get your things inside and introduce you to Mama."

His mother was in the office in back of the kitchen. "Mama, she's here!" he said.

"Who's here?" Sadie asked.

"Christine. The girl I've been writing to, and sent the money. Mose brought them out from town."

"Didn't you know she was coming?"

"No ma'am. She said she sent a telegram, but I didn't get it. They're in the parlor. Come on and I'll introduce you."

"You said they? How many are there?"

"Remember I told you about her brother? He's with her. There was no one to take care of him when their mother passed."

"Miss Christine, this is my mother, Sadie. Mama, this is Christine Pogue and her brother, Caleb."

"Welcome to the Lazy J Ranch," Sadie said. "Did you have a nice trip?"

"It was pretty uncomfortable," Christine said.

"I always thought the sleeper cars were comfortable," Trace said.

"We were in the regular car," Christine said.

"The railroad office told me the cost of a ticket, so I thought I sent plenty for both of you to have Pullman tickets. It included the meals.

"It wasn't enough," she said. "I almost didn't come."

"Maybe you shouldn't have," Sadie mumbled.

"I'm sorry. I didn't hear what you said." Christine said.

"Nothing," Sadie replied. "It wasn't important."

"Let's go upstairs, and I'll show you your rooms," Trace said.

"Mama's room is at the end of the hall. Mine is at the other end. Yours is here in the middle and Caleb will be across the hall from yours." Trace said.

"I have my own room?" Caleb asked.

You do, unless you're afraid of being alone," Trace said.

"I'm not skeerd of nothing," Caleb said.

"Good for you," Trace said. He opened the door to what would be Christine's room. "I'll bring your trunk to your room."

When he set the trunk down, she said, "There's no tub in here."

"There's one next to Caleb's room, and one in Mama's room."

"This not what I expected," she told him.

"This is Montana," he said. "We have a lot more than most. Most of the ranches don't have electricity and some don't even have water inside."

"I suppose it will be all right," she said.

"I have some chores I have to get done before supper," he said. "I'll be back in an hour or two."

"I thought you owned all of this? Don't you have people to do this?"

"I will own it all someday. Right now, it's Mama's. Ranching is hard work and dangerous. We work hard. Every day."

He went back downstairs. "She's older than I thought she would be," Sadie said. "I thought she was your age."

"She said she was."

"I'm not going to get involved, but I'm going to tell you I don't like her. She's a complainer, and I think you sent more than enough for her ticket."

"I thought so too," he said. He had never mentioned the second wire of money.

After dinner, Christine asked, "When will we be getting married?"

"I thought we would get acquainted to make sure it's what we want," Trace said.

"I didn't come all the way out here to get acquainted," Christine said. "I came to get married. I thought that was the intent of the entire advertising thing."

"Before I get married, I want to make sure it's the right thing for both of us," Trace said.

"I know of people that got married as soon as they got off the train," Christine said.

"I can't do that," Trace said. "Maybe I had better take you back to town. It's too late to go today, but I will tomorrow morning as soon as I finish my morning chores."

The next morning…

Christine took one last look in the mirror. *I almost messed this up yesterday. This place is too good to mess up.*

"Trace, Miss Sadie, I have to apologize for yesterday. I was worn out when we got into Helena yesterday. All the problems with Mama, and her funeral, then trying to decide what to do, and Caleb. Then when nobody met us, I was afraid I had taken the wrong train or had the wrong town, I was worried. I'm sorry.

"Trace, you're right. Marriage is too important to just rush into. I do want us to be happy together. Will you give me another chance?"

"I understand. Moving across the country where you don't know anyone can be unsettling to a body. Having just lost your mother had to be hard. I remember how we were when we found Papa had been killed. It was hard for us to get past, and we were living where we had always lived, so I know how it can be."

"Miss Sadie, the only kind of cooking I know is farm cooking. We raised most of what we ate, and Mama did most of the cooking until she took sick, but I will help you all I can and I'd be obliged if you show me how to cook what you're used to having."

"We raise most of what we eat too," Sadie said, "so we eat a lot of beef. I have my little garden and we have chickens for eggs and cows for butter and milk."

"The day starts early out here," Trace said. "I'm up before daylight, start a fire in the stove, and heat a pot of coffee. I grab a couple of cold biscuits, and I'm in the barn before sunup. After I finish out there, I come back in and Mama has breakfast ready, then I'm out with the hands until supper time."

"You have help don't you?" she asked.

"We have ten hands right now, including Newt. We add a couple in the spring and fall for roundup."

"Would you have the time to show me what the ranch is like?" Christine asked.

"I'll make the time," he promised. "Would you like to go?" he asked Caleb.

"Yeah," the boy said.

"Yes sir," Christine corrected.

"We'll do it tomorrow after breakfast. Do you have boots?" he asked Caleb.

"No sir."

"We'll have to get a pair," Trace said. "All cowboys wear boots."

The next morning, Trace hitched a team to the wagon and set off to show them the ranch. "We have to move the herd around to different pastures or they'll eat the grass right down to the dirt. We also have high pastures and low pastures. During the summer, we move them to the high pastures. In the winter, there's too much snow, and it's too cold in the high country, so we move them back down. We've already moved most of them down, and we'll get the rest moved in the next week or so. After that, it will be roundup time, where we get them all together and decide which ones and how many to take to market."

He stopped the wagon. "Look over yonder," he said and pointed. "There's one of the herds. Do you want to get closer?"

"Is it safe?" she asked.

"We won't get that close," he said and flicked the reins, then turned the horses in the direction of the cattle.

"Isn't anyone watching them to keep them from running away?"

"There's two cowboys with these because they were just moved. There's one on each side. The cattle won't go anywhere unless something spooks them." He stopped the wagon. Minutes later, the cowboy closest to them came to the wagon.

He pulled his horse to a stop beside the wagon. "Need something, boss?"

"No, just showing our visitors around. Clem, this is Christine and Caleb."

"That's a lot of cows, " she said.

"Cattle," Trace said. "We milk cows. These are beef. How many in this herd, Clem?"

"Between twelve and fifteen hundred. I better get back, he will be wondering what happened."

"Ma'am, it's been a pleasure." He touched the brim of his hat, wheeled his horse around and resumed his work.

"How many cows… cattle do you have?"

"Somewhere between five and six thousand. We won't really know until after the roundup."

"This is a big place," she said.

"It's not the biggest," he said. "Thunder Canyon is a lot bigger than we are." He flicked the reins and continued the tour.

Acquainted

A month after their arrival at the Lazy J, Christine accepted Trace's proposal of marriage. They were married by the territorial judge. Trace's mother and the judge's clerk were witnesses. Their wedding night was spent in the Palace Hotel.

"When are we going on our honeymoon?" Christine asked.

"This time of year, I can't be away from the ranch very long."

"Why not?" she asked.

"It's one of the two most important times of the year. It's when we make our money. It's roundup time, and then the drive to market. After that, it's breeding time. The other important time is spring roundup and calving time."

"I was really hoping to see San Francisco," she said.

"Next year, after the roundup, we'll go to San Francisco," he promised.

"That will work for me," she said, smiling. "I can wait."

* * *

Mary Catherine came home from school and found a letter on the desk in her room. Among the other news her mother wrote about was a wedding.

"Sadie told me at church yesterday Trace married a mail order bride from Ohio this past week. They are living on the Lazy J.

"I know you have exchanged letters with him since you went back. You haven't said anything about it being serious between you, so I hope it doesn't upset you."

This is a surprise. It's been over a month since the last letter, so he must have started this while he was still writing to me. I hope they are happy together. I'll bet his mother is happy about it.

That evening at supper, she told Julia about it. "Remember the man I was writing back home? I had a letter from Mama today and she told me he had gotten married two weeks ago."

"Are you disappointed?" Julia asked.

"I was glad he started writing. It meant I had another friend my age. It bothers me a bit he was writing to me while he was doing this. I hope she makes him happy."

"That was kind of sneaky of him to do that," Julia said.

"I doubt it was intentionally sneaky. I wish he had told me about it though, instead of just not writing anymore."

"It was sneaky," Julia replied. "I didn't know the mail order bride thing was still going on. There was a couple I knew back home that met that way, but they were Mama's age."

"I had never heard of it until I came to Montana. It's how Mama met Papa. They are happy together and I hope this works for Trace."

"Have you ever thought bad things about anyone?"

"I try not to, but when it happens, I ask for forgiveness."

"Girl, you are not like anyone I've ever known," Julia said.

"I don't know whether that is a compliment or not," Mary Catherine said.

"I meant it to be. What are you going to do over the holidays?"

"I'm going to get to know my family again, Then, I'm going to see how what I'm learning will apply to life on the ranch. After that, if I have time, I'm going to get some sleep."

"Mama's last letter said they have a telephone line run to the ranch now, and I'm supposed to ask Mrs. Healy if she would object to Papa having one installed in my room. Then I could talk to them instead of writing."

"I've never even seen one," Julia said.

"I haven't either, but it would be nice to talk to them more often than I can now."

* * *

"Aren't you going to church with us this morning?" Trace asked as he was dressing.

"I don't think so," Christine replied. "I was sick again and don't feel like the long ride into town."

"You haven't gone in several weeks now," he reminded.

"I can't help it," she said. "I just don't feel up to the long ride into town and back."

"I wish you would go," he said.

"I don't feel like it, and I'm not going, and that's it," she snapped.

The next morning…

Christine had one piece of bacon left on her plate when she bolted from the table and out of the kitchen onto the porch. She stuck her finger down her throat until she began gagging.

Trace heard her retching and followed her. He saw her breakfast on the ground beside the porch.

"Ugh," she said. "That's a horrible taste. I need to rinse my mouth."

He went back to the kitchen. "Mama, I think maybe I had better take her to the doctor. This has been going on for two weeks."

"Sounds to me like she's with child," Sadie said. "I never was sick with you, but I hear tell some people are sick the whole time."

"Can the doctor do anything about it?"

"Not unless they have found something new."

* * *

"Christine, Mama thinks you might be with child."

"It's certainly possible, don't you think?" she said, a coy grin spreading across her face.

"I want you to see Doctor Palmer and let him check you out."

"That's not necessary. If it weren't for losing my breakfast every morning, I would be fine."

"I would really like for you to see him. He's good. He saved my life, after the Indian raid."

"The Indians attacked the ranch?" she said, her voice showing her alarm.

"Yes, they set fire to the house, and I had two arrows in the back. I almost died from it."

"What if they come back?"

"They won't. They've all been put back on the reservation. Now, about the doctor…"

"I don't want anyone poking around and touching me in my special places except you. Would you like to touch me or maybe…" Her voice trailed off suggestively. "You can undress me if you want."

"In the middle of the day?"

"Why not?"

"What if Mama comes in and sees us."

"She probably knows what we do when the door is closed, and the lights are off."

"I'd probably be too embarrassed in the daylight," he said.

"I thought you liked that part of being married," she pouted.

"I do," he said, "it's my favorite part."

"Then show me."

As soon as he finished and left the room, she poured some vinegar from a bottle onto a cloth and cleansed herself thoroughly as she had done throughout during their marriage. *That should take care of it.*

Where's Mama?

"The stove is cold," Sadie said, when they returned from church. "I thought Christine was going to put the roast on so it would be ready when we got back."

"She must be sick again," Trace said. "I'll go check on her." He found a note on the pillow.

I can't do this anymore. This is your mother's house and will never be mine. I don't want to live in the middle of nowhere anyway. I need to be around people. I have a man who promises to give me the things I want and deserve.

I already had a husband, so we were never married. There is no baby and never was. It was all a joke. Don't try to come after me. I won't come back.

I will leave the horse and buggy at the stable.

There was no signature.

Stunned, he sat on the bed. *There must be some mistake. She wouldn't do this to me. We're married. We're going to have a baby.*

He went to the kitchen and handed the note to his mother.

Her jaw dropped as she read it. "Well, I never... I always thought something was off about her. What gets me is she left Caleb."

"What are we supposed to do about him?"

"What do you mean, do about him?" Trace asked. "We take care of him. He has nobody else. He was left just like we were. I'll have to tell him."

"Caleb, I have some bad news. Your sister has left us. She left a note saying she won't be coming back."

He didn't blink. He just looked at Trace with eyes filled with sadness. "It ain't the first time she left me. And she ain't my sister; she's my mama. Mr. Trace, my name ain't what she told you. It's Jordan."

"Who was Mr. Pogue?"

"I don't know no Mr. Pogue."

"What happened to your Papa?"

"We left him."

"Why?"

"Mama didn't like him no more. Just like you. Are... Are you gonna whip me?"

"Why would I do that?"

"For not telling you my real name."

"Would you like to go back to your real papa?"

"He would whip me."

"Did he do that a lot?" Trace asked.

"Sometimes, when I was bad."

Real cowboys don't cry, but Trace was as close as you could come without it. "We're not putting you anywhere, and you're not getting a whipping. This is your home and you're staying here with us."

"For true?"

"For true," Trace said. Now are you going to help with the chores or not?"

"I'm going to help."

"Good. I need all the help I can get. Let's go get it done. On to the barn."

Later...

"Caleb told me Christine was his mother, not his sister. His father is back in Ohio. He said they left because Christine didn't like him anymore. Then he said 'Just like you', meaning me. Their name is Jordan, not Pogue. He asked me if I was going to whip him for not telling me his real name. I tell you, it's just about the saddest story I ever heard."

"You need to go see Phil Barnes," his mother said. "This whole thing's been fouled up from the get-go. Why, I'll bet she was lying about her mother dying too."

* * *

Philip Barnes Law Office...

Trace explained the situation to Phil Barnes, who had been the Jennings family lawyer for years. He showed him the letters and the note Christine had left.

"There's two matters here that come into consideration. One is the marriage. I'm sure Judge Horner will declare it void. She perjured herself when she signed the license.

The other matter is the boy. If his father is living, then he has the parental rights. I'll present the annulment papers to Judge Horner, and I'll check on the situation with the father. Do you know his name?"

"Caleb is with Mama at the preacher's house. I'll go bring him here and you can ask him whatever you need. He's a good boy, but I think he's been mistreated. I'll be back in half an hour."

Jack and Lettie Owens home...

After the hellos were out of the way, Trace said, "I guess Mama's told you?"

"Yes," Lettie said. "I always try to look for good in everyone, but I'm having trouble finding any here."

"She played me for a fool and I acted like one," Trace said. "Phil Barnes wants to talk to Caleb. It shouldn't take long, and we'll be back."

"Caleb, Mr. Barnes is a friend of ours, and he wants to help. To do that, he needs to talk to you. All he's going to do is ask you a few questions. Just tell him the truth, and we'll come back here."

"Yes sir."

"Trace, I'm going to talk to him privately," Phil said. "I don't want him to look at you for answers."

"Caleb, go with Mr. Barnes. I'll wait right here. I promise."

Fifteen minutes later, they returned to the outer office. "Apparently nothing you were told is the truth. His grandmother didn't die and his grandfather wasn't killed in the war. They both live in Canton, Ohio. His father's name is Ray Jordan.

"I'll get the marriage papers done up today and if you wait around, you can sign them, and I'll take them to Judge Horner tomorrow.

"I'll have to write the father to determine the status of the boy. That will probably take two weeks for the letter to go both ways."

"Thanks Phil. We appreciate it."

"Caleb, tell Mr. Barnes thank you for his help."

"Thank you for your help, Mr. Barnes," Caleb said.

Phil stuck out his hand, and Caleb solemnly shook it.

"I'll be back before we leave and sign the papers," Trace said.

When Trace returned to sign the papers, Phil said, "Judge Horner will probably rule on this right away. Do you have a telephone yet?"

"Not yet, we've thought about it. I'm not sure we need one."

"The Parsons have one and they swear by it," Phil said. "Do you want me to send someone out with the news when the judge rules?"

"That's not necessary. I'll find out the next time I'm in town."

"You're not the first one, Trace. I've seen a couple of these mail order marriages go bad with and have seen both men and women at fault."

"I'm not surprised. I never dreamed anything like this could happen, but Mama was suspicious after the first letter," Trace said, "but I guess I wanted to believe it.

"I'll see you on Friday."

On Friday, Phil said "Judge Horner declared the marriage null and void. It never happened."

"But it did happen. Thanks, Phil."

CHAPTER THIRTY

Graduation

Two years later…

"Mary Catherine Parsons," the University of Nebraska dean of students read from the scroll he held.

Mary Catherine walked across the stage. "Congratulations, Miss Parsons. As the only woman in a man's field, you've done a remarkable job."

"Thank you sir," she replied, accepting the sheepskin diploma. *Who said it's a man's field?*

She rejoined the other graduates until the ceremonies were over. "Congratulations, honey," Jonas said, wrapping his arms around his daughter. "I'm so proud of you, I'm just about to pop my buttons."

"Thanks, Papa. I couldn't have done it without you and Mama."

"Nonsense," Emma said. "We didn't answer the questions. It was all you. I knew you could do it. Now we have three college graduates in the family, only four to go."

"What's next?" he asked.

"I want to go home," she said. "I want to get reacquainted with my family, then I'm ready to go to work."

"Now that sounds like a well thought out plan," Jonas said.

"It's all I've thought about for the past year," she said. "In all my wildest dreams, I never thought I would see this day," she said.

The next evening, after supper, they were sitting in the parlor. "I have one more dream," Mary Catherine said.

"What is that, dear?" Emma asked.

"I want to be a mother. I've had a perfect example, and I think I can be a good one."

"I'm sure you will be," Emma said. "Anyone in mind?"

"No ma'am."

"Whoever he is, and wherever he is, he will be a lucky man."

That evening…

"Did I tell you about Trace?" Emma asked.

"I don't remember if you did. What about him?"

"His wife packed and left while they were at church. They came home and she was gone. Sadie doesn't talk about it much, but there's something strange about the whole thing. The boy she told them was her brother turned out to be her son. She left him behind too, and he's staying at the ranch. Sadie told me about the marriage being annulled, but that's all she said."

"That is terrible," Mary Catherine said. "I can understand how the boy feels to be abandoned by his mother. He's a lot older than I was, so it probably hit him harder. What are they going to do?"

"Sadie hasn't said, and Trace hasn't talked to anyone that I have heard."

"Let's change the subject," Jonas said. "Tomorrow morning, I want to show you something."

"What?" Mary Catherine asked.

"It's a surprise. Just get dressed for a ride after breakfast."

The next morning…

"I'm ready for my surprise," Mary Catherine said.

"Wade and I put our heads together and made some changes," Jonas said.

"What kind of changes?" she asked.

"You'll see." Two horses were saddled and ready. Mary Catherine mounted the mare she always preferred to ride.

"Which way," she asked.

He pointed his horse across the pasture. "We've done some separation." The Longhorns are all together. I decided to go whole hog on your suggestion."

"Which suggestion was that? I don't remember making one."

"About the Herefords. Instead of twenty I bought two hundred Hereford bulls and we crossbred them with the Longhorns. The calving this spring was really good. He pulled up short of a group of Herefords with calves that were markedly different from the others.

"What do you think?" he asked.

"They are beautiful," she said. "How many?"

"I'm pretty sure we have between five-hundred and a thousand, which would be six or seven per bull, but it's just a guess, I don't know. At this age, you can already see the difference between these calves and the pure Longhorn calves. Way more than enough to call it a success.

"Your suggestion is going to make a big improvement to our profitability."

She blushed in the face of the praise. "I'm glad."

"Maybe I went too far, but Clint and I did the same with the Circle C, except we only did one hundred. It was your money, but in my opinion, it was a good investment."

"They estimate one bull for each twenty to thirty cows," she said, "but it's only an estimate."

"Our number is higher than that, but we have a big herd.

Do you want to ride over there?"

"I'd like to," she said.

Circle C…

"Mary Catherine," Clint said. "It's good to see you. Jonas told me you'd be back this week. Are you all finished?"

"Yes sir, they taught me all my head can handle, so they sent me home with a paper in my hand that proves I'm now educated."

"Good. We can use some education around here."

"I've been showing her the results of my experiments with our herd. Why don't you tell her what you see?"

"Sam would be proud of what has happened. The Herefords survived the winter with a loss of only two or three, and we have a nice crop of calves that are putting on weight."

"I'm glad it is working," she said.

"When are you going to move in?" he asked. "We decided to stay in our house and the big house is just sitting here waiting for you."

"I just got home, Mr. Weathers, I've never thought of moving."

"Maude has washed and stored all of Sam's clothes, so everything is ready. She's been looking forward to you being here. You're not thinking of selling are you?"

"No, I could never sell Mr. Sam's home place."

"Good. We've been hoping you'd feel that way."

"Papa, what do you think I should do about the house?" Mary Catherine asked.

"You know we all love you, and like your company. Having said that, if you're serious about the ranching business, I think you should live here and get involved in the day to day operation and record keeping. If you are not serious, then you should hire someone to live here and run the operation, or just sell it. Clint is getting to the point where he will be wanting to slow down before too many more years pass. Remember, we are the next door neighbors to you.

"When the time comes, and you have your own family, you will already have a fine place to live. Does that bother you?"

"Yes, it does, but it makes sense."

"Every parent faces the prospect that his children are going to be grown and lead their own lives. The girls will mostly move, and some of the boys will too. It's a bittersweet situation, because it means we have done a good job, but we will still miss them. You're our daughter, and you're no exception."

She brushed a tear from her cheek. "Have you talked to Mama about this?"

"No, but she's smarter than I am, and she knows it."

"I guess I need to talk to her too."

Later...

"How did your day go?" Emma asked.

"Good and bad," Mary Catherine said. "The good part was I spent all day with Papa. We went over to Mr. Sam's place and I talked to Mr. Weathers."

"The bad part?" Emma asked.

"I'm not used to being in the saddle and I'm sore."

Emma laughed.

"That's not the worst part. Mr. Weathers thinks I should move there, and Papa agrees I should either do that or hire someone to live there and run everything, or else sell it."

"What do you think you should do?" Emma asked."

"They're right. I can't sell Mr. Sam's place, but I hate the thought of leaving my family now that I'm finished with school and back home."

"We're next door," Emma reminded. "You could get a telephone, and are a ten minute ride away.

"Papa said you would say something like that."

CHAPTER THIRTY-ONE

You're Back

Christian Church, Helena…

"I heard you were back," Trace said.

"I came home last weekend," Mary Catherine said.

"How long are you home for?"

"I'm finished. I graduated last week," she said.

"You must be proud of yourself."

"I am. I worked hard, and I learned a lot. I don't believe I know this handsome young man."

"This is Caleb. Say hello to Miss Parsons. She lives close to us," Trace said.

"It's a pleasure to meet you, Caleb. You're new in town, aren't you?"

"Uh huh."

"Caleb doesn't talk much," Trace said. "Kind of like me."

"Papa told me you got some Hereford bulls. How did they do?"

"Pretty well," Trace said. "We didn't lose any over the winter and we've had some calves born. Y'all got twenty didn't you?"

"Papa changed his mind, and got two hundred. He was showing them to me yesterday."

"That many? That was taking a big chance."

"Not really. Crossed with a Longhorn, gives you some sturdy stock. They fatten up quicker, and have better meat."

"You learned about them in school?"

"We studied them. When I showed Papa the records, he decided to give them a try. It's paying off for us."

"Maybe I should have gotten more," Trace said.

"You'll be seeing a lot of them around here when word gets out unless I'm badly mistaken."

"The music has started. I had better go in. Nice meeting you, Caleb." She went inside with her family.

"Was that Mary Catherine you were talking to?" his mother asked.

"Yes ma'am. She's finished college and is back home now. You know those ten Hereford bulls I bought? It was her idea. She told Jonas about them and they bought two hundred. Said they did pretty good too."

"Did she ask about Christine?"

"No ma'am, why?"

"I'm sure Emma told her about it. You wrote her about getting married, didn't you?"

"No ma'am. I never did write her again. I just didn't see a point to it."

After the services, he approached Mary Catherine again. "Do you have a minute?"

"Sure, what do you need?"

"I wanted to apologize for just stopping the letters without an explanation. It wasn't right and I'm sorry. I had already advertised when we started writing and I should have told you. Then she came, and I didn't know what to say."

"Don't give it another thought. I'm sorry things didn't work out for you."

"Yeah, well, that's the understatement of the year. I'm grown and I'll get over it. The real loser is Caleb."

"Is he going to stay with you and Miss Sadie?"

"I hope so. Our lawyer has been trying to contact his father, but so far hasn't gotten an answer. I don't know what's going to happen."

"I'll say a prayer for him," she said. "You too."

"Thanks for understanding," he said.

"I'll never understand how a mother can leave her child. I've always wanted to believe mine had a good reason. I'm just happy with the way things turned out with Mama and Papa. Maybe it will be like that for Caleb.

"I have to go. I see Mama and Papa are in the wagon already."

"Nice seeing you again, Mary Catherine. I'll bet you're glad to be home."

"I am," she said.

In the wagon…

"He told me they are trying to get it so Caleb can stay here, but so far his lawyer hasn't heard anything from the father. I hope it works out for them.

He said they bought ten Herefords, and all of them made it through the winter, and they have calves, but didn't say how many.

"I'm encouraged," Jonas said. "These last two winters have been the worst I've ever seen. Several ranches lost over half their herds, and some cowboys died in it. We lost more than usual, but nothing like some of the others. I don't know whether the canyon sheltered us or what.

"Clint said they fared pretty well too. It drove the price of beef up when we went to market.

"Someday, we are going to start seeing local slaughterhouses and refrigerated freight cars," Mary Catherine said. "Swift Company is building their own now."

"I lost my daughter and got a cattlewoman instead," Emma said.

"No you haven't lost me, Mama, and never will, even after I move to the Circle C."

"You decide on that, did you?" Jonas asked.

"I think so," she said.

"Well, if you move, I'm moving with you," Mattie declared.

"If you do that, who is going to take care of Mama?"

"Lettie and Jonas," Mattie said.

"I'll make you a deal," Mary Catherine said. "I will have a room for you and you can spend the night sometimes, but Mama needs you to help with Joshua. Besides, you're going to be going to school before long."

"And I can spend the night with you?" Mattie asked.

"Some nights, but Mama has to say when, okay?"

"Okay," Mattie said grudgingly. "When are you going to move?"

"Probably next week. I'm going to ask Mama to help me decide what I will need to buy."

Circle C…

"Mr. Clint, do you know my mother, Emma?" Mary Catherine asked her foreman.

"I don't believe we've met," he said. "Clint Weathers, ma'am. This is my wife, Maude."

"I'm pleased to meet you, Mrs. Parsons," Maude said. "We think a lot of your daughter. We're happy she's decided to move in. We've been afraid the ranch would be sold."

"I'm pleased to meet you, Maude, and please call me Emma. Mary Catherine asked me to help decide what she will need after she moves."

"I think pretty much anything she will need right away is here, except for food. Everything is clean, and ready to be used."

"Miss Maude, I told Mr. Clint the other day, there is no way I would ever allow Mr. Sam's home place to be sold. You have a home here for as long as you want."

"Thank you, Mary Catherine. Clint told me, but I needed to hear it from you. Emma, don't worry about your daughter. We will look after her and help as much as we can."

"I don't worry about Mary Catherine," Emma said. "She's proven she is a responsible adult."

"I need to get back to work before the boss lady fires me," Clint said.

"Let me show you the house, and where things are. Bessie always took care of the house for Sam, and I'll introduce you to her too. She's a good cook, but there hasn't been the need for much of that since he passed."

"That would be good, Miss Maude," Mary Catherine said.

"What do I have to do to get you to forget the 'Miss' Maude and just call me Maude?"

"I'll try, but I will probably forget once in a while. Or most of the time."

"This was Sam and his missus' bedroom. He never changed anything after she passed."

After the tour, Mary Catherine said, "I would like to brighten up the bedroom, maybe move some of the hangings into another room. Other than that, everything looks fine to me."

CHAPTER THIRTY-TWO

Circle C

Circle C Ranch...

Mary Catherine and Clint were in the office when Bessie told Clint there was someone to see him.

"It's probably someone you don't know, so I'll introduce you," he said.

It was Trace. "Howdy Trace," Clint said.

"Howdy," Trace replied. "Mary Catherine. I'm surprised to see you here."

"Hello Trace. It's nice to see you again. How's Caleb?"

"He's good. Clint, I have a question for you. Have you thought about adding Hereford's to your herd?"

"We have some already," Clint said.

"Have you thought about adding more?" Trace asked.

"You'd have to ask the boss," Clint said, smiling.

"Who is that now?"

"You're looking at her," Clint said.

"Jonas owns the Circle C?" Trace asked.

"No, I do," Mary Catherine said.

"You?"

"Yes, Mr. Sam graciously left it to me in his will. What did you want to know?"

"Uh... I've been thinking about adding some more, and was wondering where you got them."

"Papa and Clint got them at the same place. I have no idea whether they have more to sell or not. I can probably find out from the University if they know of any available. It's where we found the one hundred-fifty we have here."

"Why did Mr. Chandler leave the ranch to you?" he asked.

"I don't have any idea, and I can't ask him, so I guess I will never know." I'll be in the office, Clint."

"What put the bee in her bonnet?" Trace asked.

"She truly does not know why he left it to her, and it was a rude question to ask in the first place.."

"I always seem to say the wrong thing to her," Trace said.

"Let me tell you something about that girl. What you see is what you get; there is no pretend about her. All she has gone through has made her a strong woman, one of the strongest I know. I'm glad she's here, and any man that tries to hurt her is going to have to go through me.

"To answer your question, we got our Herefords over in Dakota Territory, and drove them here. As far as getting more, Mary Catherine will make that decision, but my recommendation would be to gradually change the entire herd and just keep a few Longhorns for old time's sake. You can see a big difference just by looking at calves the same age."

"Please tell her I apologize," Trace asked.

"Why don't you tell her yourself? She ain't hard to talk to, just be honest with her."

"Seems like I do a lot of apologizing to her."

"Come on in if you want to talk to her. She was just telling me about some of the records she's planning to keep."

"Mary Catherine, I won't take much of your time," Trace said. "I always seem to put my foot in my mouth when I talk to you, and I want to apologize."

Flashing a smile, she said, "It's all right, Trace. I had to turn away to keep from saying something myself."

"Clint answered my questions. He mentioned you were thinking about keeping new records. You mind telling me about them?"

"Not at all. I would like to find a way to keep track of a bull's breeding record. If he's not effective, then why waste a cow's calving cycle?"

"That makes sense, but it would take a lot of time," he said.

"Maybe so," she said, "but it would be nice to know when culling your herd. The same thing for cows, their age and the number of calves they've dropped. Someday, somebody will figure a way to do it.

"That's enough business. How is Caleb doing? I think about him often."

"He's doing pretty well in school, but he's behind the others his age. I don't think they paid much attention to his schooling."

"If I'm not being too nosy, have you heard anything back about his father?"

"We did, or at least the man we thought was his father. Our lawyer wrote to one in Ohio, and the man pretty much said he had no children and to leave him alone. We're going to court and try to adopt him."

"Oh, I do hope you can."

"So do I. He's going to need a mother too, but I'm not going to try the mail order thing again."

"How old is he?"

"As near as I can figure, he's seven or eight. We know he was born in July, but we don't know what year.

"I better be getting on back," he said. He stopped at the door. "Mary Catherine, I saw a poster for a show at the Orpheum. Would you like to see it with me?"

"Trace, I would love to. Thank you for asking. When is it?"

"Next Friday. What about if I pick you up early, and we can have supper and then go to the show."

"It sounds perfect. The family is planning to stay at the house in town over the weekend, so pick me up there instead of here, and I'll stay in town. I wouldn't want to be out on the road so late at night. I'll see you then, and thank you again."

Lazy J…

"Did you know Sam Chandler left the Circle C to Mary Catherine?"

"Did he really?" Sadie said.

"She said it was in his will," Trace said. "She's living in the ranch house now. Clint thinks an awful lot of her. I asked her why he left it to her. She told me she had no idea, and went back in the house. Clint got as mad as a wet setting hen. He told me the question was rude, and how much he thought of her."

"I went back and apologized. Seems I do a lot of that with her. Anyway, she was really sweet about it and said it was all right. Then I asked to go to a show in town next Friday."

"You did? What did she say?" his mother asked.

"We're going to have supper, and then go to the show. She sounded really pleased I asked her."

"I always liked her," Sadie said.

CHAPTER THIRTY-THREE

You Won't Believe This

"You probably won't believe this, but I've been asked to a show in town. I don't know what it's about," Mary Catherine said.

"Well, don't just stand there, tell me who," Emma said.

"Trace Jennings. He came over and was asking about our herd. Clint answered his questions, then Trace came back and asked me to go with him next Friday."

"That's wonderful, honey. Are you looking forward to it?"

"Very much so."

"Does he know about you and the ranch?" Jonas asked.

"Yes, I told him, but…" A concerned look caused her to frown. "Papa, do you think that's the reason he asked me to go?"

"I wasn't trying to suggest that at all. You don't think it might be the reason do you? If you do, then you shouldn't go."

"He's a good man. He's trying to do the right thing and has his lawyer trying to find Caleb's father. He's going to court to try to adopt him. I admire him for that.

"If you don't mind, I'll ask him to pick me up and drop me off at the house in town, then I won't have the long ride home so late at night.

"That's a good idea, Mary Catherine."

Friday night…

"What is this show called?" Mary Catherine asked when Trace came to pick her up.

"According to the poster, it is called *Haverly's Circuit,* and is a variety show."

"It will be a new experience for me. The only things I've ever seen resembling a show are those green lights in the sky at night, and a couple of storms in Thunder Canyon."

"That's about it for me too," he said.

"Mama and Papa went to Paris on their honeymoon and saw several shows and an opera while they were there."

"I've seen enough of the world between here, New York and back and forth to Nebraska. I don't have any urge to travel.

"I've never been further than Cheyenne, and I don't even remember it," Trace said. "Someday, I would like to go to Texas and see if I can find the cemetery where Papa is buried."

"It would be very satisfying if you did. It's too bad he couldn't have been brought home."

"It is. I have a lot of memories with him. When I was little, he would put me in front of him on his horse. I would hold on to the pommel, but he kept his hand around my waist. This is probably uncomfortable for you. I shouldn't be telling you this."

"Of course you should. I don't begrudge anyone's memories of their parents. I wish I had memories from early on. Mine started when I got here, and they are all good, except for losing Mr. Sam."

Later…

"That was fun," Mary Catherine said. "I have never laughed so much in my entire life. Thank you for the evening.

The moon came from behind a passing cloud and cast a silvery glow around them. The street was quiet. There was no noise from the saloons at the opposite end of Last Chance Gulch. "Are you going home tonight?" she asked. "It's pretty late. I would ask you to stay at our house, but it's small and there's no room when everyone's here. I think even Pearlie May came in."

"It's okay," he said. "I might go to the boarding house or even take a room at the Palace. I'll be up early to get back to my chores.

"I would like to do this again," he said. "I enjoyed it."

"I did too. It was nice having someone to talk to. Thank you again."

She went inside. Emma was in the parlor mending a pair of Little Jonas' pants. "Did you have a nice time?" she asked.

"I really did. I thoroughly enjoyed it."

"How was it with Trace?"

"He was a perfect gentleman, and we talked about lots of things. He would like to go to Texas someday and try to find where his father is buried."

"Will he ask you again?"

"Well, he asked if I wanted to and I said yes," Mary Catherine said.

"I'm glad. You need these kinds of experiences."

"I guess Papa is already asleep."

"Probably. He went to bed half an hour ago. I wanted to get these pants mended so Jonas can wear them tomorrow."

"I can finish them if you want to go to bed."

"I'm just about finished. You go on to bed if you want to."

"Mama, what do you think of Trace?"

"He's a nice young man, though I sometimes wonder about his maturity."

"Like what?"

"He should have told you about getting married instead of just not writing."

"He apologized for that and I accepted."

"I may be wrong, so I'm not going to say anything else," Emma said.

"No, I wanted your opinion."

* * *

"Are you saving these seats for anyone? Trace asked.

"I'm saving one for Caleb. You're welcome to join us if you like."

"I believe I will take you up on that," he said.

"Since you've never been to the Lazy J, I would like for you to come have dinner with us some day."

"I would like that," she said. "Tell me when."

"I'll let you know," he said.

Dinner at the Lazy J…

"Mary Catherine, I'm glad you could come," Sadie said. "I've been looking forward to this since Trace told me about it. It's hard to believe you've never been here before."

"I don't believe I have, but I haven't done any visiting since I finished school, except to visit family."

"How do you like living alone?" Sadie asked.

"I prefer to be with my family, but Mr. Sam trusted me with his place, so I'm doing my best to take care of it."

"It was a mystery why he didn't leave it to the Weathers'."

"I was as shocked as anyone else, Miss Sadie," Mary Catherine said.

"He always was a strange old coot."

"Sam Chandler was one of the nicest men I ever met," Mary Catherine replied. "He was the very first friend I had when I came to Helena.

"Is Trace here?"

"I think he's in the barn. I'll ring the bell and let him know you're here." She opened the back door and pulled the rope attached to a bell."

"We have one of those at home," Mary Catherine said.

"Most folks do," Sadie said. "Beats yelling when you need someone."

"I guess it does."

Sadie looked toward the door. "That's him, scraping his boots. He doesn't come into my house without scraping his boots. I won't have my kitchen smelling like manure."

"Pearlie May says the same thing," Mary Catherine said. "She'll be on you like a duck on a June bug if you track her floor."

"When did you get here?" he asked.

"About fifteen minutes ago," she said.

"Ma, you should have let me know."

"You knew she was coming."

"If you'd like to see our calves, I'll take you after dinner."

"She didn't come over here to see your half breed calves," Sadie said.

"It was her idea," Trace said. "They have a lot more than I do."

"Longhorns have stood us in good stead ever since your grandpa drove them here from Texas."

"They have, but times are changing. A lot of the ranches are mixing Herefords in with their Longhorns."

"Are you going to jump off a cliff because a lot of people are doing it?" Sadie asked. "I don't like change, and we're doing just fine the way we are."

"Miss Sadie, can I help with the dishes?" she asked.

"No, y'all go on and do whatever it is you're going to do."

"Thank you for dinner, it was delicious."

"Nothing special," Sadie said. "Just old fashioned chicken and vegetables from my garden."

"Let's go, Mary Catherine, I'll introduce you to Newt."

"Is he your foreman?"

"He is and a good man too."

CHAPTER THIRTY-FOUR

A Change

"I would like to court you," Trace said, stopping the wagon near the barn.

"I don't know anything about courting," Mary Catherine said. "What do people do when they court?"

"It's where a couple decide to get to know each other and find out if they are interested in getting married to each other."

""I want to be friends, but I don't think it would work, us getting married," she said.

"Because of some of the things I said?"

"No, not really. I know you didn't mean them the way they sounded. The real reason is, I don't think your mother likes me."

"Why do you say that?"

"Didn't you hear what she said? She said she doesn't understand why Mr. Sam left the ranch to me instead of Clint and Maude. It's like she thinks I did something to make it happen. I don't understand it either, but it was rude of her to come right out and say it. She seems to flat out resent what we're doing with the cattle. What I heard was she wants to keep things the way they are."

"She isn't the one asking to court you. Anyway, she does like you. She's been trying to get me to pay attention to you since you came."

"Why haven't you?"

"I tried, and got tongue tied when I try to talk to you. I still do."

"Your letters didn't show it."

"You didn't see how many tries I threw away before I had one I could mail."

"I don't see how anyone could get flabbergasted by the thought of talking to me," she said.

"It isn't as bad as it used to be. There was a poster in the barber shop about Buffalo Bill's Wild West Show coming to town. Would you like to see the show?"

"Sounds interesting," she said. "I'm always trying to learn more about my adopted state. When is it?"

Two weeks from Friday," he replied.

* * *

Thunder Canyon Ranch…

"What's going on in your life?" Emma asked Mary Catherine.

"I had dinner with the Jennings' the other day. Trace invited me. I enjoyed it except Miss Sadie. I didn't care for what she said about Mr. Sam. She called him a strange old coot. I told her he was the first real friend I ever had.

"She is against changing the makeup of their cattle, in fact, she almost forbids it."

"That goes back a long way," Jonas said. "Papa told me about it. After Sadie's father died, her mother and Sam kept company for quite a while. Everyone expected them to marry, but Sam up and married someone else. There's been hard feelings between them ever since."

"It must go with the land, because I don't think she likes me either. There's no telling what she will say or do when she finds out what Trace did."

"What did he do?" Emma asked.

"He asked if he could court me. I didn't have any idea what that involved. He told me it's when people agree to get acquainted better to decide about marrying each other."

"I'd say that is a pretty good description," Jonas said.

"Did you court Mama?"

Emma laughed. "Yes, but he sure went about it in a strange way. First, he didn't meet my train, then he ordered me out of his hospital room. He got really mad when I put the money he sent for my train fare back into his account."

"We did have a pretty rocky start," Jonas admitted, "but it didn't take us long to work it out."

"I don't know how to answer, so I'm going to tell him he has to talk to you about it," Mary Catherine said.

Emma said, "Where I came from, the boy had to get the permission of the girl's parents before courting, so I would say it's a good answer, even though you're both past the age of needing permission."

"Before you encourage him, be sure of how you feel," Emma suggested.

* * *

The arena was crowded, and they had barely gotten settled in their places when the sounds of gunfire startled them. Thirty war whooping Indians astride bareback ponies came thundering into the arena.

Trace blanched. Mary Catherine saw his distress and touched his arm. "Are you all right?" she asked.

"That was a little too realistic," he said. "It was the way they sounded when they raided the ranch."

"I forgot about what you went through. Would you like to leave?"

"I'm all right. It shocked me at first. I wasn't expecting anything like this."

"I'm not surprised. You might very well have died that day."

"Do you think these were real?"

"They were real all right," he said. "They were Lakota's, same as the ones that hit us."

"I can't imagine what it would be like to go through something like that."

"One good thing came out of it," he said.

"What?"

"I met you."

"Nothing notable about that," she said.

"It is to me."

"Now that is sweet."

"Cowboys are not sweet," he told her.

"Oh, you," she said, tapping the back of his hand with her fingertips.

"That felt good. Do it again."

When she did, he caught her fingers, and held them. "Got you," he said.

"It would seem so. What do I have to do to free myself?"

"Say I can court you," he replied.

It was the opening she was waiting for. "It's okay with me, but you have to get Mama and Papa's approval."

"You're past the age where you require permission," he said.

"I'll never be past the point of wanting their approval though," she said. "Here they come again," she said, as a bugle sounded and a group dressed like Cavalry chased the Lakota's out of the arena.

He didn't flinch this time. "All right, I'll ask them after church on Sunday."

CHAPTER THIRTY-FIVE

Courting

Church was over and the usual small groups had formed for the last few words until they would see each other again, next week, or next month, or whenever.

Trace waited while Jonas and Silas Farmer finished their conversation. He drew a line in the dirt with the toe of his boot. Jonas was finally free.

"Jonas, I wonder if I might have a word with you?" he asked as he erased the line he had drawn.

"How can I help you?" Jonas asked.

"Sir, I've spoken with Mary Catherine, and she said I needed to talk to you and Miss Emma."

"I'm available, but I believe Emma is talking to Lettie right now," Jonas said. "What is this about?"

"I, uh… I spoke to Mary Catherine and uh… I asked if I could uh… court her. She said it was all right with her, but I needed your approval."

"Why do you want to court my daughter?" Jonas asked, enjoying the conversation.

"Well, sir, she's a nice girl. Smart girl too, and I, uh…, well, I like her."

"I have to tell you, I knew this day was coming, and I've been trying to think how I would answer. She's an innocent girl, and you've been married before, and, it's like this, you have my approval. Understand this, if you hurt my daughter, in any way, shape, or form, I'm going to land on you with both feet. You understand me?"

"Yes sir. Thank you sir. I won't hurt her, Mr. Parsons."

"See that you don't. Now, all you have to do is convince her mother, and she's headed this way." He clapped Trace on the back. "Good luck. He coughed to hide his smile.

"Miss Emma?"

"Trace how are you?" she said. "I just spoke with your mother a few minutes ago. She tells me you've repaired all of the damage to your house."

"Yes ma'am, pretty much. Miss Emma, Mary Catherine and I have been talking and I want to court her. She said I had to have your approval."

"Have you talked to Jonas?"

"Yes ma'am. He said if it was all right with Mary Catherine, and you approved, then he did too. Miss Emma, I'll treat her right, I promise."

Emma smiled broadly. "Trace, I have a great deal of love and respect for my daughter. If she wants you to court her, then you have my blessing."

"Yes ma'am. Thank you ma'am. I will treat her like the lady she is."

"Does your mother know about this?"

"No ma'am. I didn't want to say anything until after I talked to y'all. Thank you again, Miss Emma."

Later...

What did you say to him?" Emma asked Jonas.

"I scared him. I said he had better be good to her or I was coming after him. I might have also told him you would be harder to convince than I was."

"Jonas, you didn't," she said laughing.

"I might have."

* * *

"I talked to your mother and father," Trace said. They gave us their blessing. Your father was hard to convince."

"Papa's a pushover," Mary Catherine said. "Mama is the tough one. Pearlie May would be harder than Papa."

"Pearlie May?"

"She really runs things around there. I've never gotten on the wrong side of her, but I have heard her give Papa what for.

"What did your mother say when you told her?" she asked.

"I haven't told her yet. I'm going to do that when I get home. I hope she approves, and I will be disappointed if she says no, but it wouldn't stop me."

"Would you like for me to go with you to tell her?"

"It would be nice, but it isn't necessary," he said.

"I'll go with you," she said. "Is she here?"

"She's here. In fact, your mother told me they talked just before we talked."

Mary Catherine took his hand. "Let's go find her."

She saw them first. "There you are. I've been looking all over for you. Emma invited us to have dinner with them at the café. Are you going to come along or not?"

"I'm coming, but I have something to tell you first," he said.

"They're already on their way. I don't want to keep them waiting. Come along now." She turned and walked away at a quick pace."

"Mama, stop," he said, his voice firm. "I have something to tell you. I am courting Mary Catherine. Jonas and Miss Emma gave us their blessing."

"Oh for heaven's sake, I knew that," Sadie said. "Now come along. You too, Mary Catherine."

"How did you know?"

"Mothers know things. Besides, you have been for more than a month."

"I guess that puts your worries to rest, huh?" Trace said in a low voice."

"I wasn't worried, I did want her to like me though. What's next?"

"I have to learn more about you," he said. "What you like, what you don't like, anything I can learn. I want to prove I'm the right person for you."

"I guess the same goes for me then."

* * *

Two months later…

The chains creaked as the front porch swing swung idly back and forth. It's nice out tonight," Trace said. "This is the kind of night you like to see during roundup, where there's no threat of storms, and the cattle are calm."

From the area of the bunkhouse, the muted sounds of a harmonica and a guitar drifted toward them. "Is all cowboy music sad?" she asked.

"I don't know about all of it, but most of it is soft. When you're out riding herd at night you sing to them. It has to be soft so you don't spook them."

"I guess you're always tired at the end of a day out there," Mary Catherine said. "Where do you sleep?"

"Most of the time, you sleep in the open, using your saddle or a rock for a pillow, and an old blanket."

"Do you sleep in your clothes?"

"Yep, you have to be ready in case they're restless and it starts storming. If that happens, everyone is out there trying to settle them down. Other times there will be only two or three with them."

"It sounds exciting," she said.

"I don't know about exciting, but it is scary. I've seen lightning dancing around their horns. They get wild-eyed and restless. If they start running, they'll run over anything in their way, whether it's a wagon, a horse or a man."

"I guess you just get out of their way and let them go."

"You don't want to do that for a couple of reasons. It can take days to round them back up, and running takes pounds off them, and pounds are money. There ain't nothing meaner than a riled up Longhorn. I won't be sorry to see them thinned out. It's getting late. I'd better be heading home. The day starts early."

"I'm glad you came over," she said. "I've enjoyed the conversation, and have learned a few things along with it."

He swung into the saddle. "Good night, Mary Catherine. If it's all right, I'll see you again in a few days."

"Come anytime," she said. "Good night, Trace."

"Will you eat with us at the picnic after church next Sunday?" Trace asked. "Our roundup starts next week, so I won't see you for a week or two."

"The church picnics are always a family thing with us," Mary Catherine said. "Why don't you and Miss Sadie join us?"

"Are you sure it will be all right?" he asked.

"It will be. I'll call Mama and let her know."

The picnic…

Emma brought blankets to sit on, and plates for everyone. The food and drinks were placed on communal tables, and folks served themselves.

The blankets were spread beneath the cottonwood trees. Mary Catherine and Trace went to fill their plates.

"Can I sit with you?" Mattie asked.

"Honey, eat with us," Emma said, and give them some privacy."

"It's okay, Miss Emma," Trace said. "We would like for her to sit with us. Caleb too." Mattie shot her mother a look of triumph.

"Thank you. That was nice of you," Mary Catherine said.

"I meant it," he said. "I'll get the drinks. Do you want lemonade or tea?" Trace asked.

"Lemonade, please." He returned with two glasses. "Stir your finger in mine," he said.

"Put my finger in your lemonade?"

""I like it sweet," he said.

"You're being silly," she said.

"It's your fault."

"How do you figure?" she asked.

"I'm in love with you," he replied, looking her in the eye.

She blushed. "You're joking again."

"No joke. We've courted for a while now, and I would like for you to be my wife."

"Oh my," she said, patting her chest with her right hand. The statement left her momentarily breathless. Since it had not been a question, she didn't answer. After they finished eating, she said, "Let's take a walk."

"I want to take a walk too," Mattie said.

"You and I can take one later," Mary Catherine said. "I want to talk to Trace for a few minutes."

He took her hand, and they walked toward the town square.

CHAPTER THIRTY-SIX

A Question

They sat on one of the benches built around a tree. "You shocked me back there," she said

"I kind of shocked myself," he said. "But now that I've had a few minutes to think about it, it's true. You've become very important to me. I find myself making excuses to ride over to your place. You're the first thing I think about when I wake up and the last thing I think about before I go to sleep."

"Wow," she said. "I had no idea."

"Have you ever thought about why I wanted to court you?"

"Not until you told me what it was. I asked Mama what it was and she told me about the same thing you did."

"Did you court Caleb's mother?"

"Not hardly. She showed up ready to marry. I didn't like the way she acted and was ready to pay her way back. She apologized and turned all sweet and everything, so we got married. It turns out she lied about almost everything. She was Caleb's mother instead of his sister. I didn't find out about it until she was gone and he told me. She was the biggest mistake I have ever made."

"Aren't you afraid of making another mistake?"

"I was disappointed when she left, and mad when I found out about everything, but marrying you would not be a mistake."

"I like you Trace… a lot. But love? And marriage? I don't know. It would be a big step to take. I have always wanted to be a mother someday, but I've never had the first thought about being a wife."

"So your answer is no, you don't want to be my wife?"

"I didn't say that. I said I had never thought about it. Trace, I don't make things up, and I don't pretend. If you ask me something, I will give you the most truthful answer I can. You asked if I had thought about it, and I haven't. I don't know what else to say."

"There's nothing else to say," he said. "We had better be getting back."

Back at the picnic, he drifted off with a group of ranchers. The last Mary Catherine saw of him was when his wagon left.

"Where did Trace go?" Emma asked.

"I guess he went home, Mary Catherine said.

"Something happen?"

"He said something and we talked about it and then we came back here, and I didn't see him after that."

"There's more to it," Emma said. "What are you leaving out?"

Mary Catherine looked around to make sure no one was in earshot and said, "He told me he loved me and wanted me to be his wife. We went to the square to talk, and he asked again. I told him I liked him, but hadn't thought about marriage. Then we came back. I haven't thought about it, Mama. It's a big step. I don't know what love is between a man and a woman. I know I love you and Papa, and my brothers and sisters, but anyone else, I don't know.

"Did you love Papa when you got married?"

"I didn't know I did, but looking back, I probably did. He told me he loved me and asked me to marry him. I said yes, and now he is the love of my life. I love all of my children, but my love for him is different."

"How do you know you love someone?" she asked.

"I don't know the answer to that. It is probably different with every person."

"I'm all confused. I think I hurt his feelings when I didn't give him the answer he wanted, but he hurt mine when he just walked away."

* * *

Jonas saw the group of men at the corral when he rode up. He called Trace.

"What brings you to the Lazy J," Trace asked.

"I told you if you hurt my daughter, I would come after you. You did and here I am," Jonas said.

"I'm not going to fight you, Jonas."

"Who's talking about fighting. I want to talk to you about what happened."

"Nothing happened. I asked her to marry me and she said no."

"It's not the way I heard it," Jonas said.

"Same as," Trace said. "She said she'd never thought about it and didn't know."

"It must not have been important to you if you let it drop that way. It's just as well, if you don't care anymore than that, it wouldn't have worked anyway. She doesn't know I'm here, and I've had my say, so

I'll leave you to your work. I just never took you for someone that would give up so easily." He wheeled his horse around and returned the direction he came from.

* * *

Circle C…

"I did it again," Trace said when Mary Catherine came out on the porch after he hailed the house.

"I'm surprised to see you," she said. "I thought you were mad."

"I wasn't mad. I was hurt and disappointed," he said.

"Come inside, and let's talk. Would you like something cool to drink?"

"A glass of water would be good," he said. "Mary Catherine, I…"

"I want to explain something first. When I was in the orphanage, there weren't any boys around that were my age. Most of them ran away as soon as they were old enough. Believe this or not, you were the first boy I have ever talked to at any length. There were some in college, but that was in school and there was nothing after class. I've had a very sheltered life as far as social activity, especially with boys.

"I meant it when I said you shocked me with what you said. I truly did not know what to say when you said you wanted me to be your wife. I still don't. I guess I'm not very grown up when it comes to love and marriage. Remember, I've only had a family for a little over two years. Miss Lettie and Jack were the first married people I ever knew. Then Mama and Papa came along and my life changed. Then Mr. Sam passed, and left this to me, and everything changed again. I'm still just feeling my way as I go."

"Mary Catherine, now I don't know what to say. I didn't think I was rushing it when I asked you. I just want to be with you, and take care of you. What I feel for you is love, and I want you to be a part of my life. Is there a chance for the two of us?"

"I want there to be," she said. "Even with all of the people living here, it's lonely, and I'm tired of being lonely."

"That's all I need," he said.

"Would you hold me?" she asked timidly.

He opened his arms and wrapped them around her. She laid her head on his shoulder, and sighed. She raised her head, and looked into the dark pools of his eyes. His arms tightened and he brought his mouth to taste the soft warmth of her lips. She shuddered at the contact and he pulled back immediately.

"I'm sorry, I shouldn't have done that."

"No, no, it's all right. I'm glad you did. It's another new experience for me. A good one. About your question, there is a very good chance for us.

"Are we still courting?" she asked.

His voice was hoarse as he said, "Yes, we are."

"Good."

CHAPTER THIRTY-SEVEN

The Relationship Blooms

"You're in a good mood tonight," Sadie said.

"I am," he said. "It's been a good day."

"In what way? It's been the same old thing here."

"It's just been a good day for me."

"Did you go see her today?" Sadie asked.

"Yes ma'am."

"I thought you had given up."

"I'm not giving up. I'm going to marry her someday."

"Does she know that?"

"I told her."

"I may get some grandbabies yet," she said.

"You already have one," he reminded.

"It's not the same. He doesn't have Jennings blood. He can't keep our line going."

The courtship continued each Saturday and Sunday for the next two months with a trip to a traveling opera, dinner and two picnics.

Emma and Jonas invited Trace to spend the weekend at Thunder Canyon the week after Thanksgiving. "Is Mary Catherine going to be there?" he asked with a smile.

"Of course she's going to be here," Emma said. "She'd be here all of the time if I had my way."

"I appreciate the invitation, and I am looking forward to it."

* * *

The weekend...

"We're going to pick out a tree this afternoon, Mary Catherine said. "The first Christmas I was here was the first time I ever had a tree. Jonas makes a big thing of it, and the kids decorate it. Mama makes hot chocolate. It's a lot of fun. I'm too old to help them now, and I'm going to miss it.

She pointed to a corner of the parlor. "It goes in that corner. We try to get a big fat one that reaches to the ceiling."

"Since it's just Ma and me, we don't do much," Trace said. "We do have a dinner for the hands."

"Papa does that too, and I talked to Clint about it. I want to spend Christmas here, so we're going to have dinner for our hands on Christmas Eve. Christmas been an exciting time for me since I've been here."

The tree…
They took two wagons, Trace and Mary Catherine drove the one that would carry the tree.

"What about that one?" Mattie asked, pointing to a tall fir.

"Look at the trunk," Mary Catherine said. "It's all crooked. Papa couldn't get it to stand up straight."

"It's straight now," Mattie said.

"That's because it's in the ground."

"I found the perfect tree," Little Jonas announced. "Come see."

"Mine's prettier," Mattie said.

"Is not."

"Is too, huh, Mary Catherine?"

"They are both pretty," she said.

Lettie said, "I want this one. It's perfect."

"It is very pretty." Emma said. "What do you think?" she asked Trace.

"I think it's perfect," he said. Lettie beamed.

"Told you," she said.

"I'll get the saw," he said.

When the tree was loaded in the wagon, they headed home, behind the other wagon. Mary Catherine skootched as close to him as she could get.

"You made Lettie's day," she said, linking her arm in his.

"This was fun," he said. "When we have kids, I want to do the same thing."

"I do too," she said.

He stopped the wagon. "Did I hear you right?"

"You did."

"You will marry me?"

"If I'm asked," she said.

"Mary Catherine, I would be honored to be your husband. Will you marry me?"

"Yes."

"Yee Haw!" he yelled, waving his hat in the air.

Jonas stopped his wagon. When they caught up to him, he asked, "Anything wrong?"

"No sir. Mary Catherine just agreed to marry me."

Emma looked her way, and Mary Catherine smiled and nodded.

"I'm happy for you both, now we better get home before we freeze," Emma said. "We'll celebrate there."

Once inside, the coats were hung to dry out, and the hugging began. "We're a hugging family," Mary Catherine said, "so you had better get used to it."

"They's lots of hot cocoa in the kitchen," Pearlie May said. "Don't none of y'all go spilling any on my floor. Now what's this bout you goan marry up with our girl?"

"Yes ma'am," Trace said. "She has agreed to be my wife."

"Praise the Lord," Pearlie May said. "It's bout time she found herself a good man. You better treat her right or I'll have yore hide."

"You just heard it from the boss," Jonas said. I was always more afraid of her than I was Papa."

"I took your britches down times when you was bad," she said. "It wuzn't offen, cause you wuz a good boy. Now that Joshua, he wuz a handful."

"We have to have some talks, Mary Catherine," Emma said. "I'm glad you're going to be here all weekend. We have a wedding to plan."

"I don't need a big wedding, Mama. We can let the judge do it."

"Oh no," Emma said. "You don't get away that easy. You're my first daughter to get married, and we're going to have a church wedding."

"Jonas, you're going to have to make up with Mr. Hartley at the hotel. It's the only decent place in town to have a reception. It's too far for everyone to come here."

"It rankles me, but I will," Jonas said.

"We should just elope," Mary Catherine said to Trace.

"You do that to your mother and you'll be the prettiest widow in Helena."

"Papa!"

"We'll have a church wedding," Trace said.

"Now you're being sensible," Emma said.

"I'll have to order a wedding cake from the bakery, and flowers, and arrange for the reception."

"I have it in my mind already," Emma said. "I'm being selfish," Emma said. "This is your wedding, honey. What do you want?"

"What you've said sounds beautiful, Mama.
I've never even been to a wedding."

"I'll ask Lettie Owens if she will do the music. She plays beautifully. There's a room off the narthex where you can change into your wedding dress. Lettie can be your flower girl. I don't know of anyone who can be your maid of honor."

"What about me," Mattie asked. "What can I do?"

"Can she be the maid of honor?" Mary Catherine asked.

"She's a little young for that," Emma said. "I know, you can be the ring bearer, Mattie. It's an important job."

"You thought of all of this in the past hour?" Mary Catherine asked.

"Honey, I've been planning my daughter's weddings for years," Emma said.

"I wore my mother's wedding dress. I'll bet I can alter it to fit you. Let's go check it and see if you like it."

She took an old box from her closet and took the white dress from it. "Mother wore it, and so did I, now one of my girls will wear it. I hope all three of you can."

Mary Catherine covered her mouth with her hand. "It's the most beautiful dress I've ever seen," she said. "I'd be afraid I might trip and tear it or something."

"You won't. You should have seen Jonas when he saw me come down the aisle. His jaw dropped." She smiled at the memories of her wedding day."

"Mama, would it be all right if I asked Julia Bedford to be my maid of honor?"

"That's a wonderful idea. You two were pretty good friends before she graduated weren't you."

"Yes ma'am. The only thing would be her getting here. I'm pretty sure they don't have a telephone, but I have her address, and I could write her."

"It would be better if you sent her a telegram," Emma suggested. "You would have an answer quicker."

"If she agrees, I'll buy her ticket, because I don't think she could afford it."

She composed the telegram.

Marrying my cowboy. Please be maid of honor. Answer collect soonest. Love, Mary Catherine.

Three days later, an answer arrived. *Honored to. Send details. Love, Julia*

For the first time since the incident during the Indian problem, Jonas set foot in the Palace Hotel. "Please tell Mr. Hartley I would like to speak to him."

"Yes sir." It was the same clerk.

"Jonas, this is an unexpected pleasure. How can I help you today?"

"My daughter is getting married, and my wife thinks this is the only place in town suitable for a reception. I'm not sure I agree with her, but I do like to make her happy. I have two questions."

"What are your questions?" the manager asked.

"Can your facility handle a reception as large as this is likely to be?"

"Will we be catering?"

"Yes."

"We can handle it. Your second question?"

"My entire family will attend the reception wherever we decide to hold it. Will they be treated with dignity and courtesy?"

"Yes sir. I will personally see to it."

"All of them, and you know what I mean by all of them."

"Yes sir."

"My wife will contact you with the details," Jonas said. "One other thing, I want the best of everything."

"You will get it. I would like to offer, with the hotel's compliments the use of the Presidential Suite for the happy couple."

"I will tell my wife."

"It is a pleasure to be doing business with you again," Hartley replied.

"Just don't mess it up."

.

CHAPTER THIRTY-EIGHT

A Bump in the Road

"We haven't talked about where we will live after we're married," Mary Catherine said.

"The Lazy J is my home, and it's where we will live," Trace said.

"The Circle C is my home," she said. "The Lazy J is your mother's home and always will be as long as she lives."

"It's the wife's place to live with her husband."

"I agree with you on that, but it doesn't mean we should live with your mother," she said. "A wife should be the lady of the house, and I wouldn't be if we lived there. You can't have two ladies of the house."

"I have a ranch to run," he said.

"So do I," she said.

"Clint Weathers runs the Circle C," he said doggedly.

"That's debatable. I own the ranch, and I make the financial decisions. He probably does more than Newt does for you, but this is a larger operation."

"Well, I say we live on the Lazy J."

"Then we have a big problem. You're not my boss and never will be. You don't get to make all of the decisions."

"It's a woman's place to do what her husband says. Before he went off to the war, Pa was the boss, and Ma's place was to take care of him and me."

"In our home, Mama and Papa are partners. She makes some of the decisions, and he makes some. The rest they make together. It's the way I want my marriage to be."

"I don't feel that way," he said.

"If that's the way you feel, then I'm sorry. Now, I think you had better go before this gets any worse."

"Are you saying you don't want to marry me?"

"Not at all, I am saying if you're looking for a laundress, a cook and a housekeeper, then you need to look for someone else. I am not the kind of person you want to marry.

"I guess that's it, then," he said.

"It doesn't have to be," she said, "but it sounds as if you have made a decision."

* * *

The Lazy J...

Trace moved his food around on the plate, but had only taken a few bites.

"What's wrong?" his mother asked.

"Mary Catherine is being stubborn," he said.

"About what?"

"We were talking about where we would live after the wedding, and she says she won't live here."

"What else did she say?"

"She says you can't have two ladies of the house, and this is your house and always will be."

"She's right. It is mine."

"Well, I have a ranch to run, and I have to be here to run it."

"She does too," Sadie said.

"Clint runs her ranch."

"He's her foreman, just like Newt is the foreman here. When you were in the hospital, we didn't shut down until you got back."

"I am going to be in charge, just like Pa was."

"If you think I didn't have a say in what went on around here, you're badly mistaken. About the only thing I didn't have a say in was him going off to war, and you saw how that turned out.

"That girl is uncommonly smart, and is wise beyond her years, especially when you consider she didn't have parents to show her the way. I'll say this, if you let this girl get away, it is going to be the darkest day of your life."

"Then you hold with all the dumb ideas about being partners and everything?"

"I do, and the man she finally marries up with will be very lucky. It's a shame it isn't going to be you."

Thunder Canyon Ranch…

"I need to be around my family," Mary Catherine told Emma. "Is it all right if I stay here a couple of days?"

"Of course," Emma said. "Am I right in assuming you and Trace have a problem?"

"Yes ma'am. We were discussing where we would live. He insists on the Lazy J and I don't want to. It's Miss Sadie's home. Then we went off into the husband is the boss and the wife is to do as he says. I just said if that is the kind of wife he wants, he needs to find someone else. He left and didn't look back. You should cancel the arrangements for the wedding. I'll let Julia know."

"Is that what you want?" Emma asked.

"No, but it seems to be what he wants. Did you and Papa have problems like this?"

"Two or three times," Emma said.

"What did you do?"

"I waited for him to come to his senses," Emma said.

"What if he hadn't?"

"Then I would be teaching in Helena, Cheyenne, or Denver. Look honey, marriage is good when it's for the right reasons, and when you both love and respect each other, but if you have any doubts, hold off until you're sure. It's hard enough out here without complicating it with a miserable marriage."

"I'm sure you're right. What do you suggest?"

"Don't make any rash decisions while you are emotional about it. Wait a week or so."

"Do you think a week will make any difference?"

"The Lord created the earth in six days. I have a feeling Sadie has had a similar talk with him."

The Circle C...

"She's not here," Clint told Trace.

"Did she go running home to mama?"

Clint's eyes turned cold. "Boy, I flat don't like your attitude. She was upset when you left here the last time, and I don't like seeing her that way. I suggest you go back where you came from and stay away from here until you can act like a gentleman and treat her like the lady she is."

"What did she say?" his mother asked.

"She wasn't there. I think she went home."

"The Circle C is her home. Maybe she went to see her family. It's what I would have done if I had a family. I wish we had kin close, instead of a bunch of smelly cowboys."

"You're all taking her side," he complained.

"I don't know who you mean by all, but there shouldn't be a side to take."

Broken

"The Jennings boy is here and wants to talk to you," her foreman told Mary Catherine.

"I'm too busy to talk to him," she said. Clint smiled and winked at her.

He gave Trace the message. "I'll wait, Trace said.

"It could be a long wait," Clint said. "Things piled up while she was gone."

"It's all right. If you don't mind, please tell her I'll wait, no matter how long it takes."

"I'll give her the message."

Later…

"I didn't know you were still here," Mary Catherine said when she walked out onto the front porch.

"I asked Clint to tell you I would wait no matter how long," Trace said.

"He did, but I thought you were long gone by now. What was it you wanted to talk about?"

"I wanted to tell you I'm sorry for what I said the other day."

"I think you were saying what you felt. There's nothing wrong with a person saying how they feel. What you want just isn't something with which I can live."

"You're calling the wedding off?" he asked.

"I asked Mama to cancel everything."

"I'm sorry you did that," he said.

"Mama suggested I give it a week before doing anything. She also said marriage is good, if you love and respect each other, but if you have doubts, then you should not do it because you will be miserable. I have serious doubts."

"What do you want me to do?"

"I can't answer that," she said. "If I told you what to do, then I would be guilty of the same thing you did."

What are you going to do?" he asked.

"I am going to keep doing what I have been doing. I asked my friend from college to be my maid-of-honor, so I'm going to ask her to come anyway, and maybe stay a while here with me."

"Mary Catherine, I am sorry," he said.

"So am I," she said.

* * *

Mary Catherine was waiting at the station when Julia's train arrived. "I can't believe you're finally here," she said. "It's been so long, and I really appreciate you coming anyway."

"I was really shocked when you said you had called off the wedding. What happened?"

"I'll tell you all about it later. Do you have a trunk?"

"Yes."

"Slim, this is Julia Bedford, a friend from college. If you point it out, Slim will get it into the wagon. It's about a forty-five minute ride. Did you eat on the train?"

"I did. I'm good," Julia said.

"You look good. Teaching must agree with you. My mother is looking forward to talking to you about your experiences. She's planning to start teaching again next year."

They passed under the arch over the gate and were on Circle C land. "We're almost there," Mary Catherine said. "We'll see the ranch house pretty soon."

"Where do you want the trunk? Miss Mary?"

"Upstairs in the middle bedroom, Luke."

"Miss Maude, this is Julia. Maude Weathers, Julia. She takes care of me."

"I'm pleased to meet you," Julia said. "You've taken over my job. I took care of her in college."

"We all love Mary Catherine, and she's no problem at all."

"Where is everyone?" Julia asked. "I was looking forward to meeting your brothers and sisters."

"They're at home," Mary Catherine said. "This is my place."

"Your place? You own this?"

"I do. When I was living at the nunnery and working in the hospital, I met a dear old man, who had broken his leg…" She looked up, "Sorry Mr. Sam… whose horse broke his leg. He didn't sleep well and I spent a lot of time in his room at night talking to him. When he passed away, he left everything to me. The ranch, the house, the cattle. All of it. Miss Maude's husband is the foreman. Anyway, after I graduated, I moved here. I see Mama often and I talk to her every day."

"Miss Maude, will you and Mr. Clint eat supper with us? I want him to meet Julia."

"I'll tell him. Thank you."

"Is there anything else, Miss Mary?" Luke asked.

"No and thank you, Luke. I appreciate it."

They were alone. "Now tell me, what happened with your cowboy?"

"He had some ideas about a wife's role in a marriage, and who was the boss. He insisted we live with his mother on their ranch. I told him what I wanted it to be like, and he didn't agree, so I asked Mama to cancel everything."

"So it's all over?"

"I don't know. He says he loves me, and I like him, and probably even love him, but I am not going to be his maid and servant."

She told her about keeping him waiting almost two hours. "He asked what I wanted him to do. I told him I didn't have an answer. It's something he has to figure out for himself." She looked up as the back door opened. "Here's Maude and Clint. You will like him. He's like a father to me, and a good cattleman. I hope he never leaves, but Mr. Sam took care of him too, so he doesn't have to work if he doesn't want to.

"Mr. Clint, I want you to meet Julia Bedford. She lived down the hall from me when I was in college. Julia's family has a farm near Omaha."

A grin spread across his weathered face. He looked down at the petite Julia, and put his forefinger to his eyebrow. "It's a pleasure, Miss Julia. We're glad you were able to make it."

After supper, Mary Catherine called her mother. "Julia made it in okay. We'll come over tomorrow morning if it's okay... We'll see you then. Love you."

They sat in the parlor exchanging what had happened until late in the evening.

The Visit

The next morning, they drove to Thunder Canyon. Pearlie May was the first person they saw. She hugged Mary Catherine to her ample bosom. "How you doing chile?"

"I'm doing okay. You've heard me talk about her, now you get to meet her. Julia Bedford, meet Pearlie May. She runs things around here.

"I have heard all about you, and finally get to meet you," Julia said.

"Where is everyone?" Mary Catherine asked.

Mr. Jonas and Little Jonas is at the barn, Miss Emma and the girls is in the parlor and I think Josh is taking a nap. Finely. He bout wore me out chasing him this morning. He into everything."

Emma was giving the girls lessons in the parlor.

"Mama, look who I brought."

"Julia, it is so good to see you again. My goodness, you've gotten even prettier."

"Thank you, Miss Emma, it's always good to see you too. I love your home. Mary Catherine told me you did most of the decorating yourself. It's beautiful."

"Would you listen to her?" Mary Catherine said. "She didn't say anything about my house when we got in yesterday, and here she is raving about yours."

"I was too flabbergasted to say anything when I found out it was yours."

"Meet my two beautiful sisters, Mattie, and Lettie. This is Julia, my friend from college."

The always direct, Mattie asked, "Are you going to spend the night?"

"No, Mary Catherine said, "but if it's okay with Mama, you can go back with us."

"May I? Please, Mama, please, oh please?" Mattie pleaded.

"Since you asked so nicely, yes you may," her mother replied.

Mattie said. "Are you about ready to go now, Mary Catherine?"

"We just got here, give us time to visit," Mary Catherine said.

"You're teaching now?" Emma asked.

"Yes ma'am. I'm in my second year."

"What level?"

"Elementary, the middle grades."

"I taught first grade in the Helena school, and loved it," Emma said. "We're going to start up a community school somewhere on the ranch for the youngsters in the area. It will save the long ride into Helena every day. I hope it will encourage some to keep their kids in school. I expect we'll have ten to twelve students."

"Julia, you could teach here," Mary Catherine said. "Why don't you move here? Mama told me they pay more than most places."

"Have you seen Trace recently?" Emma asked.

"He came over the other day and asked what I wanted him to do. I told him I couldn't answer that."

"Couldn't or didn't want to?" Emma asked. "There is a difference."

"I didn't want to. I told him what my feelings were. He has to figure out what he wants for himself."

"And if he doesn't?"

"It would be too bad for both of us."

"Did you know he came here and asked my advice? It was probably the same day he talked to you."

"What did you tell him?"

"I'm not going to answer that. You'll have to figure it out for yourself."

"I hate it when my words are thrown back at me," Mary Catherine said. "I'm going to show Julia around, Mattie, get what you're going to take with you together, and we'll leave after dinner. Be sure to take a dress for church, and you can come back home with Mama and Papa afterwards."

"Mattie really cares for you," Julia said.

"No more than I love her. My first day here, she gave me one of her dolls because I told her I had never had one."

"Was that true?"

"I try to always tell the truth," Mary Catherine said.

"Sometimes the truth can hurt," Julia said.

"It can. Let's go find Papa."

"Papa, you remember Julia?" she asked.

"Of course I remember Julia," he said, leaning the hay fork against the stall. "Welcome to Thunder Canyon."

"This handsome man is my brother, Jonas," Mary Catherine said.

"It's good to see you again, Mr. Parsons. I'm always happy to meet a handsome cowboy, Jonas."

"When did you get here, and how long are you going to stay?" Jonas asked.

"I got in yesterday, and I don't know how long I'll be here," Julia said.

"I'm trying to talk her into moving here," Mary Catherine said.

"You'd like it here, except maybe the winters," he said. "The people are friendly and good neighbors."

"We have some pretty rough winters in Nebraska too."

"Papa, Pearlie May said to tell you dinner will be ready in half an hour."

"We'd better get washed up, and get the bottoms of our boots cleaned off," he said to his son. "We don't want to get on the wrong side of her."

Jonas and Emma chose to seat their children at the large table in the dining room with the rest of their family and guests rather than in the kitchen.

"I'm an only child, and the only other times I came close to eating with this many people was in the boarding house," Julia said. "It was a lot different. I love this."

"We like for the kids to be a part of what we do," Emma said.

Pearlie May, I'll help you," Mary Catherine said, and began gathering the dirty plates.

"I'll help," Julia said.

"You girls go on about your business," Pearlie May said.

"We're going to help. You did enough work fixing such a good meal."

"All the time," Pearlie May said to Julia. "She heps me all the time. I don't ast her, she just do."

"She used to help Mrs. Healy when we lived in the boarding house too," Julia said.

Later...

"Trace came over again," Clint told her when they stopped in front of the barn.

"Did he say anything?" Mary Catherine asked.

"He asked when you'd be home, but I didn't know, so he didn't wait. He said to tell you he was going to town tomorrow and would stop by to see if you need anything.

"How long are you going to keep that boy dangling, Mary Catherine? You know you're going to marry him sooner or later, so why don't you let him off the hook? You're just wasting your time and his."

"You know more than I do," she said, because I haven't decided."

"I doubt you've ever played poker, but there's an expression that would be good advice for you... don't overplay your hand."

"What is that supposed to mean?" she asked.

"Think about it," he said. "You're the smartest woman I ever met. It'll come to you."

"I need to meet this man," Julia said. "He sounds sweet."

"I'll introduce you when he comes the next time."

"Good. Maybe I'll move here after all," Julia said.

Mary Catherine looked at her friend. She didn't know whether she was kidding or not.

The next morning…

Trace hailed the house. "It's Trace," Mary Catherine said to Julia. "Come on and I'll introduce you."

"Miss Sadie, Trace, meet Julia Bedford, my friend from college. Julia, this is Trace's mother."

"Pleased to meet you," Sadie said. "We would love to have you both over for dinner while you're visiting."

"That's very kind of you. I don't know what plans Mary Catherine has made for us. Trace, she has told me about you. It's nice to be able to put a face to the name," Julia said.

"Are you the same one Mary Catherine was going to…"

"Yes, I'm the same Julia," she said.

"Mary Catherine, we're going to town and I thought I would see if you needed anything," he said.

"Clint told me," Mary Catherine said. "It's very thoughtful of you to offer, but we just stocked up when Julia came in yesterday."

Sadie cleared her throat.

"I guess we had better be getting on down the road," Trace said. "We want to get back before dark." He flicked the reins to get moving.

"He seems like a nice man," Julia said.

"He is," Mary Catherine said.

"I'll take him if you're going to throw him back on the pile."

"You leave my cowboy alone."

"Maybe you should remember what Clint said last night about overplaying your hand," Julia said. "I remember a quote from college that said, 'The woman who hesitates is lost. I'm just saying…'"

CHAPTER FORTY

Reflection

The next morning…

Maude Weathers had breakfast ready for the table when Mary Catherine came in, rubbing her eyes. "Are you sick?" Maude asked. "Your eyes are blood red."

"I didn't get much sleep," she said.

"Y'all stay up talking?"

"No ma'am."

"Then it's the Jennings boy. Clint told me he's been coming over here looking like a lovesick calf."

It was a rueful smile. "You're right," Mary Catherine said. "Between you, him, and Julia, you're all right."

"You want some advice from an old woman who should be minding her own business?"

"If you have any words of wisdom, I'd certainly appreciate them."

"Two words," Maude said. "Marry him. He comes from good stock, and he'll treat you right. That's more than two, but they're all important."

Julia came in. "Is that coffee I smell?"

"It is. There are cups in the cabinet, and cream in the icebox," Maude said. "Breakfast is ready."

"Good, I could eat a horse."

"This is a cattle ranch," Mary Catherine said. "We don't eat our horses. We ride them."

"Behold," Julia said. "She stirs. She's not dead after all. Have you been rubbing dirt in your eyes? They are as red as any I've ever seen."

"You should see them from my side," Mary Catherine grumbled.

"What's wrong?"

"You said some things that kept me up all night."

"Good. My coming here is not wasted after all."

"I'm going to make sure Mattie is up and dressed," Mary Catherine said. "After we eat, I want to go for a ride. I'm going to fix this."

One of the hands hitched a mare to the buggy. Mary Catherine took the reins and headed for the Lazy J.

"I just love this country," Julia said. "It is so beautiful. I was looking through the window as the sun came up over the mountains this morning. I've never seen anything as pretty."

"Actually, Thunder Canyon is prettier because of the canyon, but we'll hold our own against any other place. Some of the tallest peaks have snow almost all year round."

"How large is the ranch?" Julia asked.

"I don't know exactly, sixty thousand acres or so. Thunder Canyon is a lot larger. If you add this one to Trace's, Thunder Canyon would still be larger, but we're doing all right. We have between around six and seven thousand head."

"That makes my head spin," Julia said. Someone's coming," she pointed to a moving cloud of dust."

"It's probably Trace. The Lazy J is just a couple of miles ahead." Mary Catherine said. She stopped the buggy and waited.

It was Trace. "Where are you girls headed?"

"Coming to see you. We need to talk."

"I had the same idea," he said. "Do you want to go to our place or back to yours?"

"It doesn't matter," she said. "But yours is closer. Let's go there."

"Mattie, how are you?" he asked. "I haven't seen you since we got the Christmas tree."

"Fine. I'm spending the night with Mary Catherine."

"I know she's going to enjoy having you," he said. "I'll meet you back there." He spun his horse around and returned in the same direction, but stayed off the road to hold down the dust.

Mary Catherine kept the horse at a trot, letting Trace get there first. Sadie was standing on the porch, shading her eyes when they drove up.

"Come in," she said, and led them into the parlor. "Would you like anything?"

"I just came to talk to Trace," Mary Catherine said. "They came to keep me company."

"Use the office. You'll have some privacy in there. It's off the hall at the end. Mary Catherine. Thank you, I didn't know what to do."

"No need to thank me. I should have never let it go this far."

"For what it's worth, I think you did the right thing. I should have done the same thing with Cort. Maybe he would have cared enough not to go off to war."

The talk…

"Can I say something first?" Trace asked. "I'm ready to live wherever you want to live. Ma told me it wasn't always the way I thought it was with Pa.

She always let him have his way. She thinks things might have been different if he had talked to her about it before joining up."

"That's a heavy load for her to carry around," Mary Catherine said. "There's never a good age to be a widow, but she was way too young.

"I still feel the way I felt before," she said, "but we should have tried to talk it out, and I should not have left you sitting on the porch the way I did. It was rude, and I don't like the idea of being a rude person."

"What do you want me to do?" he asked.

"We, Trace, not me, not you, we. What do we need to do? We have to talk to each other, and not leave the other person to figure things out themselves."

"I went over to talk to your mother for advice."

"I know. She told me, but she wouldn't tell me what you talked about. She said I had to figure it out for myself. I have, and I want to be your wife, but I think we should live on the Circle C. We have to work this out together."

"What I want to do is make you happy," he said. "I would like for our family to be like your family."

"That is my dream too," she said.

"Then we'll make it come true. Will you marry me?" he asked, and wrapped his arms around her.

"Yes, I will," she said.

"We need to let your mother know," he said.

"Let's start by telling those here," she suggested.

"Good idea."

Sadie was in the kitchen with Julia and Mattie. Each had a slice of pie in front of them. Mattie and Julia had milk while Sadie had a steaming cup of coffee.

They walked into the kitchen holding hands. "I asked Mary Catherine to marry me again and she said yes.

"Ma, first, I want you to know we will be living on the Circle C."

"Good for you both," Sadie said. "I knew you would come to your senses and do the right thing."

"I'm going to be the ring bearer," Mattie said.

"Yes, you most certainly are," Mary Catherine said, hugging her sister. "You will be our only ring bearer."

"And I'm going to catch the bouquet and find me a cowboy to marry," Julia said.

"Good luck on getting one that will leave Montana," Mary Catherine said. "I'll call Mama when I get back home and see how soon we can have the wedding,"

The Final Plan

"We figured it all out, Mama. Trace proposed again and I said yes again. Now I need your help in picking a new date."

"Honey, I can't tell you how happy that makes me. I thought you could work it out if you left the emotion out of the discussion. As far as the date, I didn't cancel anything. If you hadn't worked it out, I would have cancelled it Monday.

"Your dress is ready. What about Julia? Is she going to be able to stay?"

"Yes ma'am, and she has something to wear also."

"Then we're good to go as planned. I'll recheck with everyone to make sure."

* * *

Meeting at Thunder Canyon…

"Here's the plan Mary Catherine and I have come up with," Emma said. "We will be staying in town this weekend. On Friday, there will be a rehearsal at the church and a dinner afterward for the wedding party.

"The ceremony will start Sunday afternoon at three. Mary Catherine, Julia and I will be at the church by one-thirty. There will be a hairdresser to fix our hair, and we will all get dressed in the room off the narthex. After the actual ceremony, we will reassemble at the hotel for the reception.

"Following the reception, we will scatter to wherever. The happy couple will go to their accommodations. Those will not be common knowledge.

"Trace, you and your mother can set your own timetable.

"Any questions?"

There were none.

Circle C Ranch…

"Mr. Clint, I know you and Miss Maude plan to be there. If anyone else is interested, they are welcome to attend. For those who do attend, I would like them to sit with my family."

"That's mighty nice of you. I have one request. Can you just call me Clint, and leave off the mister?"

"I'll try," she said, "but don't count on it."

* * *

After the rehearsal ended, and everyone knew their roles, they made their way to the Palace for the rehearsal dinner.

"I appreciate the efforts you all put in to make the rehearsal a success, Emma said. I'm sure Mary Catherine does too. We are a truly blessed family, and we've had no bigger blessing than to have Mary Catherine as our daughter.

"Wade, Gabby, we're glad you could join us. Maude, Clint, the same goes for you. Thank you for taking care of her for us."

Clint nodded and put two fingers to his brow.

"Mary Catherine has something to say. Honey, the stage is yours."

Mary Catherine stood, and looked around the room, meeting each person's eyes. "I will probably wind up crying before this is over, but I owe each and every person in the room a great deal for all the kindnesses you have shown me.

"I left New York City at the age of seventeen with nothing. I had two dresses. There were forty-five orphans and three nuns on what was called the Mercy Train by the Foundling Home. It was better known as the Orphan Train. After we arrived in Helena, there were two small children, both girls, and me that had not been adopted. The Sisters at Saint John's allowed me to stay there. I worked in the hospital, usually at night until one day, I was blessed to meet the most beautiful lady I had ever seen. She was kind and gave me some good advice when I went to her for help. She also introduced me to my mother."

She paused and walked to Lettie Owens. "Miss Lettie, thank you. You were a godsend to me when I needed help and advice, and I love you for it." She hugged Lettie tightly.

She wiped her eyes. "I knew I wasn't going to be able to do this without crying. While I was still working in the hospital, I met a kind man, truly a gentleman, Mr. Sam Chandler. I spent quite a few nights sitting by his bed listening to his tales of Montana and the danged horse that broke his leg." She looked toward the ceiling. "Mr. Sam, I know you're watching. I love you and hope you approve of what we're doing with your ranch.

"That brings me to Mama and Papa, and my brothers and sisters. No girl could ever hope to have a nicer family, and better parents. I love all of you and can never, ever tell you how much I appreciate you for making me a part of your wonderful family. I love you all.

"The first day I was at the ranch, I met Mattie and Lettie. Mattie was playing with a doll. When I told her I had never had a doll, she went to the toy box and came back with another doll."

Mary Catherine held the object Julia handed her. "Mattie, I still have Miss Betsy. I took her to college with me, and she has a place in my room just as you have a place in my heart. I thank you for your generous gift. I will treasure her always, and I love you." She hugged Mattie. "Thank you," she whispered.

"Clint, Miss Maude, thank you for all you do for me. I appreciate it.

Lastly, Trace. My dear Trace, my partner. We had some bumps in the road, but we've handled them. I love you and will make you the best wife I possibly can."

Jonas stood. He cleared his throat. "How in the world can anyone follow something like that? Mary Catherine, you have been a joy and a blessing to us. We love you as much as any parent can love a child.

"I'm here to tell you, this girl has more guts and grit than any person I have ever met. The things she has faced boggles my mind. She is kind, sweet, giving, and thoughtful of others. I am proud she calls me Papa.

"Trace, if you don't treat my girl right, I'm coming after you, and it won't be pretty when I catch you. Honey, come give your Papa a hug."

Trace stood by Mary Catherine's chair, took her hand, and asked her to stand with him. With his arm around her shoulder, he said, "Mary Catherine, I can't do this without leaning on you. I don't have the words to say the kind of things you said. I want you to know I will be there to hold you when you're sad, and laugh with you when you're glad. I'll be there to pick you up when you fall, but I think you will be doing a lot more picking up than I will. I love you honey." He bent his head and kissed her.

Emma stood, and opened her arms to embrace Mary Catherine. They hugged tightly. "It falls to me to have the last word," she said. "We all are better people for having met you, Mary Catherine. Our Dear Lord truly gave us a bounty when He sent you to us, or us to you. I would like to ask Jack to close with a prayer of thanks.

"Thank all of you for coming."

Jack stood, and stretched his hands toward heaven, and began, "Our gracious Heavenly Father…"

CHAPTER FORTY-TWO

The Wedding

The Parsons had many friends, and they flocked to the church for Mary Catherine's wedding. Fifteen minutes before the wedding, it was standing room only. The Circle C cowboys, with their hair slicked down, hats in their hands, and their jeans freshly washed surrendered their seats to others. They went to the back of the church and leaned against the wall as the sanctuary filled.

In the room on the left side of the narthex, Julia and Emma were dressed and helping Mary Catherine get her dress to hang straight. Emma adjusted the veil, and handed her the bridal bouquet. "Are you nervous?" she asked.

"Very, but I'm ready," Mary Catherine said. "Thank you both for everything."

The music started. "Julia, we had better take our seats. Jonas is at the door waiting for you. You are truly beautiful, honey."

Thanks, Mama, you too Julia."

They left through the opened door. "I remember the first time I saw that dress," Jonas said. "Your mother was about half way down the aisle before I saw her. She was so beautiful, I could hardly stand waiting at the altar. You are going to knock them dead."

She took his arm. The first three notes of The Wedding March boomed out, and their first steps put them in the aisle leading to the altar,

One of the cowboys on the back wall put his fingers to his mouth to whistle, but was jabbed in the ribs by the one standing next to him.

Slowly, measured step by measured step, they made their way toward the altar. Whispers of appreciation came from their guests.

Trace met them at the edge of the altar. Jonas placed Mary Catherine's hand in his. "Remember what I told you," he whispered, and took his seat.

They stood in front of Jack.

After an opening prayer, he asked, "Who gives this woman to be wed to this man in Holy Matrimony?"

"Her mother and I do," Jonas said.

"We are here today to unite this couple in Holy Matrimony. In marriage we not only say, I love you today, but also, I promise to love you for all of our tomorrows.

"Trace and Mary Catherine, in the days ahead of you, there will be stormy times and good times, times of conflict and times of joy. In the stormy times, remember the sun is always just beyond the clouds.

"I remind you that marriage is a precious gift, a lifelong commitment, and a challenge to love one another more completely, each and every day.

"Please join hands and look into each other's eyes.

"Trace, with this understanding, do you take Mary Catherine to be your wedded wife to live together in marriage? Do you promise to love her, comfort her, honor and keep her for better, for worse, for richer, for poorer, in sickness and in health, forsaking all others and to be faithful only to her, so long as you both shall live?

Trace's response was loud and clear, "I do."

"Mary Catherine, with this understanding, do you take Trace to be your wedded husband, to live together in marriage? Do you promise to love him, comfort him, honor and keep him, for better or worse, for richer or poorer, in sickness and in health, forsaking all others and to be faithful only to him, so long as you both shall live?"

Softly, Mary Catherine said "I do." Her voice was low, and sweet.

"Trace and Mary Catherine, you have consented together in holy matrimony before God, and have pledged your vows to each other, in accordance with the laws of the Territory of Montana and the tenets of the Church. With the authority of God's Word, and the great Territory of Montana, it is with great joy, I now pronounce you husband and wife.

"You may seal your vows with a kiss."

It was the first time their lips had touched today. The kiss was brief and tender.

"Please face your friends and guests," Jack told them.

"Ladies and gentlemen, I present to you, Mr. and Mrs. Trace Jennings."

Lettie began the recessional music. The newlyweds turned and began to walk back down the aisle. Mary Catherine stopped at the first row, and hugged each member of her family, including Pearlie May, who was seated at the end. She told each of them, "I love you."

On the other side of the aisle, she hugged her mother-in-law.

Halfway down the aisle, she stopped, her face lit with a bright smile. "Sister Anne! I'm so glad you came. The other guests were surprised to see the bride in glistening white, being hugged by the nun in her black habit.

On down the aisle and into the bright sunlight of a perfect Montana day.

"Miss Mary Catherine," one of the Circle C said, "we'd better be getting on back to the ranch. They just wanted me to tell you congratulations, and thank you for inviting us."

"Luke, that's so sweet of you," Mary Catherine said. "Before you go, I want you to stop at the hotel and fix up some food to take with you. We'll be there in ten minutes. Tell the others how much I appreciate y'all coming."

"I have never in my life seen cowboys do anything like that," Trace said.

"Those boys would ride through a prairie fire for your wife, Trace," Clint, who had just joined them, said. "By the way, how many of your hands are here?"

"Just Newt."

"Now there's the difference. Mary Catherine told me to tell ours that anyone who wanted come, could. All of them, but two were here, and they were tied up at the last minute. Maude wants to help out at the hotel, so we're going on over there. We'll see you there."

"I think I have just been told you're a better rancher than I am."

"Clint didn't mean it that way," she said. Hooking her arm in his, she said, "Some more people are waiting to talk to us."

"You maybe, not me."

"Now you stop that. We're a team, remember. What's said to one is said to both. By the way, that's from the book of Matthew in the Bible."

"I never heard it before."

"Come on, I'll prove it." Tugging on his arm, she led him to Jack Owens. "Mr. Jack, would you tell my husband about the passage that says, '*Inasmuch* as ye *have done* it *unto one of the least of these my brethren*, ye *have done* it unto *me*.'"

"It's from Matthew, Chapter 25. This girl knows her Bible."

"The nuns we had for teachers saw to it," Mary Catherine said. "I didn't get my knuckles rapped as much as some, but I got enough to teach me a lesson."

* * *

Before leaving for the reception, Mary Catherine approached Julia. She handed her the bouquet. "I've got my cowboy. Go find yours."

Julia brushed the tears from her eyes. "I'm going to try."

Mary Catherine took Trace's arm and left for the reception.

The reception hall was arranged with tables and chairs with a buffet set up against one wall. Before they ate, Mary Catherine and Trace went to each table and thanked the occupants for coming.

"I'm so proud of her, I could bust my buttons," Jonas said.

"I am too," Emma said. "We are doing it right, and she will too."

Two hours later, Jonas pulled Trace aside. "There's a back hall the hotel people use to bring food from the kitchen. At the end of the hall, is a set of stairs. The Presidential Suite is on the fourth floor. Your things are already there. Don't make a big thing of it when you leave. We would like for you to have dinner with us at the ranch tomorrow. You take care of my daughter." He shook hands with Trace, clapped him on the back and said, "Now go to her."

The Presidential Suite…

"I love you, Mary Catherine, and I will try not to hurt you."

"It's all right. Mama talked to me about it, and I know what to expect. Trace… I love you too."

The End

Epilogue

The next morning…

"I was worried about last night," Mary Catherine said. "I was afraid I wouldn't be good for you."

"Well, it was a waste of time worrying. Things couldn't have been better," Trace replied.

"Thank you for being patient with me."

"My pleasure," he said, and grinned.

"You're bad, Trace Jennings. Bad to the core. Let's have breakfast and go let the folks know we survived."

Thunder Canyon…

The family was gathered in the parlor. "Emma and I have been talking about a wedding present," Jonas said. "If you could go anywhere you wanted, where would it be? We went to Paris, but what would be your choice?"

Trace looked at his wife, but didn't say anything at first. Then he said, "We will need to talk it over. We're a partnership now."

Mary Catherine smiled. *He's learning.* "My choice would be Texas, and search for Trace's father."

"I don't think so," he said. "Let's talk about it later."

The years to come…

The honeymoon did not come until the next year when Trace and Mary Catherine traveled to Texas. They were able to locate the cemetery in which the dead from the last battle in the Civil War were buried, he was able to place a wreath on his father's grave.

Mary Catherine and Trace had three children, two sons and a daughter. Judge Horner ruled in favor of their petition to adopt Caleb. He also agreed to the request for a name change to Jennings.

Julia Bedford made the decision to move to Helena after her contract with the school district in Nebraska was fulfilled. Her story will be told later.

Mattie Parsons frequently spent the night on the Circle C.

Emma and Jonas raised their children to be thoughtful and giving.

Mary Catherine kept the graves of Sam Chandler and his wife clean and weed free. They decided they would make it their final resting place when the time came.

If you enjoyed On a Train Bound for Nowhere, I respectfully ask you to leave a favorable review on Amazon. They determine the success or failure of a book in a competitive genre.

You might also enjoy these two sweet historical romances:

Saving Amelie's Marriage
Abby's Love
Susan's website

ABOUT THE AUTHOR

Susan Leigh Carlton lives just outside Tomball, Texas, a suburb twenty-six miles northwest of Houston. She began writing and publishing on Amazon in August of 2012.

Susan observed the eighty-third anniversary of her birth on April 17th. She says, "I quit having birthdays, because they are so depressing. Now I have anniversaries of my birth. Susan and her husband celebrated their fifty-first wedding anniversary on April 16th, 2017, the day before her birthday.

She said, "One of the joys I get from writing is the emails I receive from readers that have read and liked my books. I even like the letters that are critical of the writing because it means the writer cared enough to take the time to write.

Visit Susan's website at
www.susanleighcarlton.com and sign up to receive advance copies of the first chapter when I start a new book.

Your honest reviews on Amazon would be appreciated.

Susan's Website

53808497R00213

Made in the USA
San Bernardino, CA
28 September 2017